SAY U PROMISE

...AGAIN!

A Hood Tale

By

Ms. Michel Moore

ISBN 0-9769991-2-9
LCCN-
FIRST PRINT- JULY 2006

SAY U PROMISE PUBLICATIONS
PO BOX 38162
DETROIT, MICHIGAN 48238
www.sayupromise.com

This novel is a work of fiction. It is not meant to portray or depict any real persons, living or dead. Any references to locales and events are a product of the Author's vivid and wonderful creative imagination.

Cover Layout: Marcus Margerum-MSGRAPHICS6.com
Photos: S. Darnell, D. Johnson
Models: Charday & Chyna

THIS NOVEL IS DEDICATED TO

MY COUSIN

OTHELLO LEWIS SR.

"BOO"

"COME OUT THE RAIN AND DRY OFF!"

♥♥♥♥♥♥♥♥♥♥♥♥♥♥♥♥♥♥♥♥♥♥♥♥♥♥♥♥♥♥♥♥♥

Special Thanks

To the Creator for blessing me with an understanding Mother, Jean Fletcher.

John, My one true backbone in the game. When no one else has me, you do.

Charday, Do ya thang! It's all love.

The readers who patronize my bookstand 'HOOD BOOK HEADQUARTERS' Thanks for 4 always stopping by.

All my people at La Salle Bank, especially La Don, Antoine and Thomas!

My Hood…LINWOOD!!!!!!

Brother Nati at Afrikan World Books in B-More and my friend and brother in the Urban Game, Sidi, holding it down in the heart of Harlem, USA. THANKS!!!!!!

TO ALL THE LOYAL

READERS

WHO WAITED FOR THIS NOVEL

TO HIT THE STREETS…

THANK YOU FOR YOUR

PATIENCE

AND

WORDS OF SUPPORT.

Ms. Michel Moore

CAUTION

IF YOU DIDN'T READ

'SAY U POMISE!'

YA ASS MIGHT BE LOST

IN THE MIX…

SO DON'T BLAME ME!

OLD NEWS

Fatima and Bro.Rasul drove both of the girls to the airport to catch the red eye flight. They said their farewells at the gate and boarded the plane.

"Don't worry London. You'll be safe when we get to Dallas. Storm and his boy Deacon have got that town on lock!"

Kenya was trying to ease her sister's mind, while she herself was a nervous wreck. When they landed and got their luggage, Kenya tried to call Storm's cell phone and once again it went straight to voice mail. She was starting to get beyond worried.

"Damn, why isn't his ass answering? He better not be fucking around with one of those Island Bitches!" Kenya mumbled under her breath

"Is everything all right?" London asked her sister. She looked directly in Kenya's face and could tell that it was a problem.

"Yeah, I was just trying to call Storm. He must not be back in town yet. It ain't a big deal."

Kenya didn't know how she was going to break the news to him about London. After all, she had been lying. Well sort of. He always thought her Uncle was the only family that she had but bottom line, it was time to face the music. Storm didn't have a choice. He would have to accept London and she would have to accept Storm and his lifestyle. Kenya tried not to worry as they took a taxi to her and Storm's condo.

When they drove up, Kenya saw all the lights on inside the house. She made a mental note to cuss Storm out for leaving all the lights on. He was the main one complaining about the bills.

"Well, this is it! I can't wait for you to see how I decorated it!" Kenya leaped out the cab. The driver sat the bags on the curb and pulled off. Kenya and London picked them up and made their way up to the door. "Wait to you see it London. It is nice as hell!" Kenya stuck her key in the door, pushed it open wide and went inside.

"Oh my God! Oh my God! Oh nooooooo........!"

Welcome Home

Kenya and London stood in somewhat of a daze. London was totally confused while her sister was completely shaken up. Both girls turned looking over their shoulders to see if they could try to stop the cab driver who just dropped the two of them off. Unfortunately he had already pulled down the block on his way back to the airport in search of another fare for the night, leaving the pair all alone and on their own. The only thing they could make out was his brake lights as he slowed down bending the corner of the quiet gated community that Kenya and Storm called home.

"Oh my God!!! Oh my God!!! Oh shit!" A stunned Kenya repeated in a loud panic filled voice.

"I'll be damned! What in the hell happened in this place? Storm! Storm! Oh my God Storm!!!"

Kenya yelled out her fiancee's name, as her twin sister London's jaw fell open almost dropping to the ground. "I can't believe this bullshit!" Her eyes were stretched open wide and filled with tears as she quickly glanced around her once perfect gorgeously designed living room.

"Storm! Storm!" She shrieked, still standing frozen in the doorway with her knees weakening by the second and her lips trembling from fear. "This is a nightmare London."

"Kenya what went on in here? How did this occur?" London quizzed interrupting her sister's apparent emotional breakdown. "This is awful."

They couldn't believe their own eyes or hardly stand the nauseating aroma that caused them to almost throw up. London reached over grabbing her sister's hand tightly as they hesitantly made their way completely into the high priced condo leaving the custom carved wooden door unlocked and open just in case they needed to make a quick escape.

Considering what the pair had just been through back home in Detroit and the condition of the room neither Kenya nor London knew what to expect with each passing step that they took. It was burning hot in the condo. Kenya raised her hand to the control panel turning off the heat that was on full blast causing the walls to sweat and each girl to become drenched in perspiration.

First all the lights in the house being left turned on, the heating system on the nut and her house destroyed. What else was next? What else could possibly go wrong? Kenya was terrified and needed her man.

"Storm! Baby are you here?" She pleaded. "Are you at home? Please answer me!"

London darted her eyes around her twins' home. She looked at the huge painting hanging over the fireplace that was crooked and peeling. Next she focused her sights onto the damaged wine colored leather furniture as well as the completely destroyed crushed coffee table. Despite the terrible mildew odor that filled the room and the mess that surrounded them, London could tell that Kenya once had the room organized and magazine worthy.

The newly laid plush wall to wall white carpet was now soiled with debris and soaked with filthy water. Their shoes were wet submerging into the floor making squishing sounds. The ceiling was caved in exposing the floor support beams of the upstairs rooms, along with a constant flow of water still causing chaos.

"Listen Kenya, from the look of things it seems as if your so-so brain challenged brilliant boyfriend must have left the water running somewhere in the house. He must be the smartest man alive. Kenya girl, you are so lucky to have a man like him." London snickered at her twin.

"Damn London, college did teach ya' lil behind one thing!" Kenya put her hand on her hip. "To be a real smart ass!" She wiped the dripping sweat off her forehead, rolled her eyes and waved her hand in London's face. "And FYI, he's not my boyfriend! Remember the ring! Remember this here ring heifer!"

The tension that was first felt when they walked in was broke briefly by the girls clowning each other.

"Okay 'Miss I Got The Ring', why don't you go upstairs and see where all this water is coming from. I'll open some of these windows and let some fresh air in here?"

"You mean go upstairs all by myself?" Kenya pouted. "You must be insane or something!"

London laughed at her sister. "You so big and bad! Why don't you go by ya' dang gone self?"

"Stop playing so much and come on." Kenya yanked her sister by the arm and they both headed toward the staircase.

The closer they got to the top of the condo stairs they could clearly hear the sounds of water running. The floor was much more damaged than the downstairs, causing the twins to lean on each other for support so they wouldn't slip or fall. The horrible smell was getting worst and the water more infested with debris.

"It must have been the fish tank that overflowed." Kenya finally reasoned with herself. She started feeling some- what relieved at the thought that all this bullshit, was nothing more than a misfortunate accident. "That's the only water that could be flowing. Maybe the pump broke or something."

"Yeah, you're probably right Kenya. That's got to be it. That's the only reasonably explanation."

As they got to the edge of the den door and pushed it open, the odor worsened. The heat that was trapped inside hit them smack dead in the face. "Oh dang!, It smells like the fish are already dead." London twisted her face turning up her lip.

"Well listen. I'm gonna run in my bedroom and get the telephone number to the Condo Management so they can send someone out here. You see if any of them are still alive." Kenya tightly placed her hand over her nose and mouth. "I'll be right back. Storm is gonna be pissed the hell off. He put a lot of dough off into that fucking aquarium."

Kenya left her sister standing in the hallway as she disappeared into her bedroom.

◎

"This is so freaking gross." London thought walking into the room searching the wall for the light switch. She felt the side of her loafers being filled with water and bent down to roll up her pants legs that were dragging along the floor making each step more grimy than the last. The fish tank was over on the far side of the spacious room and making a terrible grinding sound. London headed over to investigate and hopefully solve the source of the problem.

◉

Kenya made it to the side of her and Storm's bed and sat down on the edge. She opened the night stand drawer grabbing the card with all the Management's contact numbers on it. As she quickly scanned down the list, she heard more water flowing from one of the bathrooms. The two baths that were connecting from the bedroom were designed differently.

Kenya's was old fashioned with a sink and tub that was porcelain with antique fixtures. It reminded her of her Grandmother's house. On the other hand, Storm's private bathroom had a shower that had a beveled three-color glass door and a sunken custom designed walk- in tub that could comfortably fit at least two people.

"I know Storm's crazy self ain't leave the water on in his spot!" Kenya huffed as she leaped to her feet bolting into the bathroom. "If he did, then that's his ass! I swear to God!" When Kenya ran in she lost her balance from all the water on the floor and slid scraping her arm on the way down.

"Ain't this a bitch." She mumbled angrily. "Now my clothes are ruined and shit! He's gonna straight up replace my outfit! Trust and believe!"

Sure enough the water was turned on full speed in the tub and had over flowed. The room smelt just like raw dirty rotten stanking ass sewerage. Kenya was almost in tears again as she tried getting up and slipped back down in all the filth.

Instead of walking over to shut the water off, she decided to crawl. It would be much easier than trying to stand up. So on her hands and knees, drenched, slimy and covered in God knows what Kenya cursed the love of her life as she tried to maintain her composure and crawl.

"I'm gonna flat out kill that motherfucker Storm when I see him. How could he be so careless?"

◉

London neared the corner of the room and started to hyper ventilate at the sight of the huge aquarium and what was inside. Her entire body was shaking uncontrollable and she became dizzy. She opened her mouth to yell out her sister's name, but no sound was coming out. London grasped for air holding her chest while backing up slowly.

"Kenyaaaaa!…..Kenyaaaaa!" She stuttered, finally getting the words together. "Come here quick! Hurry up! Please hurry!" London's heart was pounding and seemed as if it was going to jump out her body. She ran out the room and stumbled into the hallway. Her system broke all the way down and she couldn't hold back any longer. She threw up all over herself and the already filth soiled carpet. "Kenya! Kenya!" She continued to plead while wiping her mouth with the sleeve of her shirt.

London's shouts of fear were interrupted by a constant assault of Kenya's high-pitched screams. She followed the sound of her twin sister's voice down the hall, in the bedroom and finally into the bathroom.

"Kenya! Kenya! You have to hurry and come with me." London yelled loudly. "You need to see this!"

When she rushed in, she had the same misfortune of Kenya, sliding across the floor, pass the sink and toilet, landing flat on her back. London was now next to a sobbing, scared and in shock, Kenya, who couldn't do anything but point her trembling finger. Sitting up, London reached for her twin.
"What is it Kenya? What are you trying to say?"

No words came out her sister's mouth as she continued to point. London took a deep breath preparing her self and peeked over into the bathtub taking a long hard stare. London felt as if she and Kenya were co-staring in a bad horror movie considering all the bad luck that was following them around.

OH SHIT

"Who is this Kenya!" London demanded to know after seeing a body floating in the tub. "Do you know this man? Is this your boyfriend?"

Kenya was hysterical and shaking. She was in a trance like state and seemed not to comprehend anything that her sister was asking. The unthinkable was now happening to them all over again, another dead body at their feet. After crawling through the toxic mess and leaning over to turn the knob, London found the totally nude, dead, decaying, bloated body ass up under water. And to make matters even worst, it had been decapitated.

"Please Kenya. Listen to me!" London grabbed her twin's shoulders and shook her hard. "Kenya do you hear me? You've got to snap out of it! It might be somebody still in here. We need to get out of this place and call the police!"

London was getting no response from a zombie like Kenya and could only think of one thing to do. So with one of her wet hands London raised back with all her strength and knocked the cow walking shit out of her. "SMACK!" The sound was so loud it woke Kenya up out her trance. London rubbed her stinging hand and repeated her first question. "Is this Storm!"

"Naw that's not him. I'm not sure who that is!" A red faced Kenya screamed somehow making it to her feet running out the bathroom. When she got into the bedroom, she ran over to the closet getting one of the many guns that were stashed all around the condo and put one up top. "I don't know what the fuck is going on. I need to find Storm! He'll know what to do!"

London was hot on her sister's heels and kept the questions coming one after another.

"We should get out of here! We should call the police! Are you sure that isn't Storm?" London stared at Kenya and waited for the answer.

"What in the fuck is wrong with you? I just said that ain't Storm!" Kenya was now getting pissed about this nightmare. "Don't you think I know my own Man? Head or no head! And fuck calling the damn cops! You must be out ya' rabbit ass mind. How would we explain this bullshit?"

Pulling her by the arm, London forced her angry twin down the hall. "Come with me Kenya. I need to show you something that might help you figure out exactly who that could be floating in your tub."

As the girls cautiously walked into the den, Kenya slowly eased over to the fish tank.

"What the fuck! Oh hell naw!" She was standing face to face with a head submerged in the corner of the aquarium. Its eyes were half eaten and mutilated by the few fish that were left swimming in and out of its mouth. A familiar letter 'A' custom designed, yellow diamond earring was glistening through the dirty water. She recognized it immediately as one of three that she, Deacon and Storm wore to represent Alley Cats. Kenya ran back over to the doorway falling into her sister's arms. "Why? Why?!!!!!"

"Do you know him Kenya? Is that Storm?"

"Damn bitch! What the fuck is wrong with you?" Kenya snatched away. "That ain't no motherfucking Storm! Now stop asking me that dumb shit!"

London knew that Kenya was in shock so she let all of her disrespectful comments go. "Well who is it then? Do you know? Can you tell?"

"Yeah I know." Kenya's face was full of sorrow. She put her head down holding the huge gun tightly in her small hand. "It's Storm's boy Deacon. They were supposed to be together when they left town." Kenya started to let here tears pour. "I'm scared London! I'm really scared!"

London hugged her twin trying her best to console her. "We need to call the police Kenya. We need help. Who would do something like this?"

Kenya looked at London with a dumb expression and replied. "Probably the same ass holes who were trying to get at you for that P.A I.D bullshit! That's the only thing I can think of." Kenya found it hard to believe. "Who would do something as treacherous as cut off a human's head. What have you done?"

"Yeah all right, but I don't understand. What would your boyfriends' friend have to do with me and my personal business?" London fired back.

"Who knows!" Kenya wiped her tears away. "But one thing is for sure. It's no way in hell we can call the cops to find out that answer."

"Okay then Kenya. What's the game plan?"

"I'm gonna call O.T. He'll know what we should do and hopefully he's heard from Storm."

"Who is O.T.?"

"That's Storm's little brother. He's running Alley Cats for Deacon and Storm while they're out of town."

"What's Alley Cats?" London quizzed.

"That's the club that Deacon and Storm own."

"Well Sis, you mean the club that Storm's owns now. Don't you?"

"Damn London, that's some real fucked up shit to say!" Kenya glanced at the bedroom door getting chills thinking about Deacon's headless body, as they passed on the way downstairs. "But yeah, I guess you're right. It is Storm's now."

London shrugged her shoulders following her sister out on the front porch. They moved their luggage to the side and sat on the bottom stair as Kenya pulled out her cell phone.

"I've gotta make this call to O.T., so we can get some damn help!" Kenya fumbled with her phone.

"Okay, I know he's Storm's brother, but what is he, a detective or something?" London questioned her twin wondering what was coming next. "Can he help with an deceased headless corpse in a tub? Just what kind of people are you out her affiliating with?"

"Damn London! Stop asking me all of them question and let me make this call!"

"Okay, sorry to annoy you! Go ahead and call him."

With her heart beating overtime she nervously dialed O.T.'s number. After about four or five rings, Storm's grumpy voiced brother answered.

WHAT DA THE HELL

"Yeah speak on it!" O.T. was angry and pissed off by being disturbed out of his sleep. "And you better make da shit it quick!"

"Hey O.T. this is Kenya."

"I know who it is." He mumbled. "What you want so damn early in the morning? A nigga like me just got in the bed good and shit."

"Have you talked to Storm yet?" Kenya held her breath and waited for his response. She prayed to God that he would say yes.

"That's why you called me?" O.T. yelled. "You blowing up my phone cause you can't catch up with dude? Come on now Kenya that's straight up foul!" He was fed up with her and her constant calling.

"O.T., I'm sorry to wake you up, but this is an emergency. Have you spoken to him or not?"

"Naw, what's wrong? What's the deal? I ain't talked to him or Deacon since they left."

"Oh my God!" Kenya closed her eyes crying softly.

"Oh my God what?" O.T. sat up in the bed and started to panic. "What the fuck is wrong?"

Kenya's voice was cracking as she spoke. "I need you to come over here as soon as possible!"

"What the fuck is wrong?" He repeated putting bass in his tone. "Stop playing with me and let me know!"

A sound asleep Paris, under the blanket next to O.T., immediately jumped up startled by his loud boisterous demands. "Who is that?" She mouthed.

"It's Kenya! Something is wrong and shit!" O.T. was fuming as he shook his head at his girl. He quickly turned his attention back to the phone conversation with Kenya. "Listen, can you cut the games out and give a brother a damn clue?"

"I can't tell you over the phone." Kenya wined. "I need for you to just come over here now. Hurry!"

"I'm on my way Kenya! Just sit tight!"

She closed her cell phone, dropping her head. The reality of the situation was setting in for Kenya.

O.T. had just confirmed that Deacon and Storm left town together. Now she couldn't get in touch with her man and poor Deacon was dead as a doorknob. Whatever the explanation was could only mean trouble.

◎

O.T. and Paris pulled up in front of the condo doing damn near a hundred miles per hour. Paris slammed down hard on the breaks, of her triple black Chrysler 300M, causing the tires to come to a screeching sudden halt. Leaping out the car before it came to a complete stop, O.T ran up the walkway to see Kenya crying and another girl with her arm around her. By the time he got close the other girl raised her face to meet his.

"What the fuck!" He had a puzzled look on his face as he turned back and forth. "Who the fuck?" O.T. shook his head in disbelief as Paris made her way to the group.

"Kenya?" Paris questioned. "I don't understand."

They both looked like they had seen a ghost.

"Yeah, me either!" O.T. raised his eyebrows.

Kenya stood up wiping her face leaving her twin sitting on the stair.

"Hey Paris. Hey O.T., I know yall confused and I'm gonna explain all of it later, I promise, but something awful done happened."

O.T. like Paris couldn't take his eyes off of London. He was listening to the words come out of Kenya's mouth, but was in a daze. This was some Twilight Zone type of bullshit to him.

"This is my twin sister London. She lives back out East in Detroit." Kenya explained. "She's gonna stay with me and Storm for a little while."

"You got a twin? All this time and you didn't tell me? I thought we was better than that!" Paris felt insulted and betrayed by her best friend. "What was the big hush- hush secret?" She asked while taking her time giving London the once over.

"Ain't this some shit! Do my brother know about this?" O.T. threw both his arms up in the air in a harsh rage. "Damn Kenya! Your ass is straight up out of order! You must be on crack or something!" London sat with a stern expression of amazement.

"Listen O.T.,.. I " Kenya tried her best to defend her deceitful actions before he continued speaking, stopping her in mid-sentence.

"Matter of fact, I know motherfucking well this ain't the damn emergency?" He spit on the grass and raised his tan colored untied Tims onto the step next to London's leg.

Kenya's hand rubbed her forehead. "Damn yall, I know I was wrong for not mentioning it but…,"

"But what?" Paris cut her off. "You forgot? It slipped ya' mind all the times we done hung out?"

London was completely thrown off also, that her own identical twin sister had somehow conveniently chose not to acknowledge her very existence to these 'people' whom she had been living with for months. She would surely deal with that issue later, but for the time being, London had enough of them beating up her sister with all the questions and stepped in to intervene.

"I sorry that you two seem to have some sort of a problem with her having family, but I think there's a bigger dilemma that we all have to deal with in there." She rolled her eyes pointing towards the cracked door. London's first impression of Kenya's friends and so-called great life was not impressive.

O.T. and Paris followed the twins into the destroyed home pulling their shirts over their noses to shield the overwhelming eye stinging stench.

"What happened in this bitch?" O.T frowned as he reached in his waistband snatching out his pistol.

"Paris was stunned, staying close to O.T. when she saw the awful condition inside the condo.

"Come on upstairs O.T." Kenya sighed.

"What's up there?" He asked before bracin' up on the grip of his shiny chrome handle 9mm.

Kenya begged him. "Please just come with me. I couldn't explain what's up there for a million dollars. Plus you wouldn't believe me anyhow!"

O.T. turned to go with Kenya. "Let's roll!"

Paris was right behind him. "You should stay down here with me." London suggested to her gently grabbing her by the arm. There was no need for Paris to have to see first hand the heinous sight of

Deacon's badly tortured body, let alone the whole aquarium thing.

Kenya sympathetically looked at her friend, urging her that London was 100% right. It would be much better for her to stay in the living room. Paris hesitantly agreed, standing silent next to London on the wet carpet, as they watched Kenya and O.T. navigate their way up the stairs. London got a slight chill in the muggy living room in anticipation of what Kenya and him were about to encounter.

"What's up there?" Paris broke the ice out of curiosity staring at London. "Can you tell me?"

"Trouble!" London replied glancing up towards the stairs trying to remain calm. "Trouble!"

◉

"Okay Kenya. What in the hell is the big surprise you got for me?"

"You'll see O.T. just follow me." Kenya led him down the hallway into her and Storm's room.

"Ahhh...fuck! The smell is getting worst!" Still holding his gun tightly he looked down at his new boots that were now ruined from all the water.

"It's in there." Kenya had broken down into tears as she tilted her head towards the bathroom door. She wanted him to go in there alone and check it out. There was absolutely no desire for her to want see Deacon in that state ever again.

"OH SHIT! OH FUCK! HELL NAW!" Kenya could hear O.T. stomping his feet yelling at the top of his lungs. "What the fuck happened?! Oh hell naw! Kenya! Kenya!" He ran into the bedroom where she was standing with tears flowing. "Where's his fucking head! Who the fuck did this?" He was confused and running around the room. "Where is my fucking brother? Tell me Kenya! Tell me!" O.T. demanded snatching her up by the collar. "Where the fuck is he at?!"

Kenya was having trouble breathing as she unsuccessfully struggled to get loose from his grip. "You're hurting me O.T." She managed to say. "Let me go." He came back to earth and apologized. "Damn Kenya, I'm sorry, but this shit is foul. I don't know what the fuck is going on." He walked away from her and looked back in the bathroom once more. "What about my brother? Is he in here too?" He dropped his head swallowing extra hard holding his gun down at his side as he paced. The wrong answer would cause him to bug all the way out.

"Naw O.T., I haven't heard from him ever since I flew back to Detroit. I've been calling his cell phone and it keeps going straight to voice mail."

A relieved O.T. raised his face to look at Kenya. "Do you know what went down here?"

"Nope. Me and my sister came home and the house was like this." Kenya blew her nose with one of Storm's wife beaters that was lying across the bed. "When I got up here to see where the water was coming from, I found Deacon in there."

"I can't believe this bullshit!" O.T. put his gun back in his waistband. "Whoever did that shit is ruthless as hell! Where's dude's head at anyhow?"

Kenya and him stepped out into the hallway.

"Go in the den and look in the fish tank."

"Yeah right!" He frowned dialing his brother's number. "Come on now!"

"I'm not playing. Go see for yourself."

"This is wild!" O.T. took in all the damage done in the condo as he walked in the den door with his cell phone up to his ear. By the time he came out he was sweating bullets and fanning in front of his face.

Paris and London were waiting at the end of the stairs as Kenya and O.T. came into view.

"What was it?" Paris quizzed her man seeing that he was looking distressed. "Is it bad?"

"Yeah, shit is fucked!" He softly touched Paris on her cheek. "We gotta figure this out quick!"

All the girls stood silent in anticipation of what O.T. had in store. Out of the two brothers, he was no doubt the irresponsible one. Kenya knew O.T. was a flat out fool, but for now, he was their only hope. She and him took turns blowing up Storm's cell phone in hopes that he would pick up and shed some sort of a light on all this madness.

While they waited, O.T and the three girls sat down on the stairs of the porch coming up with a scheme to try to get Deacon's body and head out the crib. Until one of them talked to Storm and knew exactly what the deal was, they thought it would be much better to keep Deacon's brutal murder on the down low. If the shit hit the fan out in the streets that Deacon was dead and Storm was missing, it would be pandemonium. The different crews around town would think it would be their chance to try to take over drug territory that Storm and his fellas had worked so hard to pump up. O.T. had no thoughts of giving them that opportunity. That meant the four of them would be on their own in this awful mess. Repeatedly getting her fiancee's voice mail was causing a red eyed Kenya to have a nervous breakdown from worry as the anxiety built.

◎

"What could have went wrong?" O.T. wondered out loud, as he had the girls collecting every sheet and blanket they could find. "As soon as we get this body up out of here, I'm gonna call that hoe ass nigga Royce. He was suppose to be with Deacon and Storm when they left."

O.T. drained all the water out the tub as well as the aquarium. Deacon's torso was bloated and water logged making it extra heavy. Putting on two pairs of the rubber gloves that Paris had ran and bought from the corner store, he tried lifting the body up by him self, but it was no use. O.T. then instructed a reluctant London and Paris to put on gloves to help him. They both quickly came to his aid. He yelled for his soon to be sister-in-law but, by that time the usually 'scared of nothing' Kenya was of no fucking good, to any of them or her self. She was curled up on the edge of the bed rocking back and forth with one of Storm's shirts in her arms.

The newly formed trio wrapped the body first in a sheet, then in two fluffy comforters. Paris found several old telephone cords out of the closet so they could tie Deacon snug. London had a box of garbage bags, which she doubled up. Holding the bags wide open, she turned away as O.T. dropped the slimy grotesque head inside.

Paris opened the garage of the condo pulling her car all the way in parking it next to Kenya's. When the door was shut and the coast was clear London, Paris and O.T. struggled to drag the body out. On the count of three, they lifted Deacon, throwing him into the trunk. The weight caused the new car to bounce downwards to the garage pavement.

" O.T., we need to get cleaned up and at least get this blood off of our clothes." Paris suggested. "We don't want to get pulled over in this neighborhood."

"I've got 9 motherfucking reasons none of these white Rodney King ass beating son's of bitches betta not fuck with nan one of us!" O.T. raised his shirt up revealing his pistol as well as his wash board Abs that he spent hours working out to achieve. "But you right, I'm gonna go back upstairs and get some of Storm's gear to throw on. I'll grab one of Kenya's track suit's for you, all right Baby?"

"Thanks Boo." Paris leaned over giving him a quick kiss on the lips. "Hurry up okay? I don't want Deacon's blood and the rest of those fluids to leak through that blanket and stain the trunk carpet."

London stood back amazed at the calm and coolness of the couple. It was as if they encountered this type of bizarre occurrence on a daily basis. *"What has Kenya gotten me into?"* She pondered silently. *"One day I'm at school working towards my degree, the next I'm tangled up in covering up two murders."*

After washing their hands getting themselves looking somewhat half way decent, O.T. and Paris were ready to roll and cautiously drove off trying to look as inconspicuous as possible. This was the one time, if any, that the Bonnie and Clyde duo didn't need to get pulled over by the cops. The two of them would dispose of the body, while O.T. left his new partner in crime, London in charge of getting Kenya's panicked grief stricken ass together. Maybe London could get her sister to postpone her sudden hysterical breakdown and relax so that they could figure this mystery out.

Now was definitely not the time for any of the three to punk out and fold. If ever there was a night that a person had to think and react with their mind and not their heart, this hands down would be that night.

It Just Got Real

Kenya was all cried out and walked down the stairs to find her sister trying her best to salvage whatever she could from the lower level of the home.

"Hey chick." Kenya sniffed pushing the redial button on her phone. "Is O.T. back yet?"

"Oh please, stop it! Don't you think you would have heard that loud obnoxious Negro?" London barked going from room to room.

"He's not that bad girl!" For the first time since they had returned from the airport, Kenya gave her twin a slight grin, holding the phone to her ear.

"I feel sorry for his girlfriend and anyone else that has the misfortune to spend any more than ten minutes in his presence." London went on making wise comments pertaining to O.T.'s off beat character. "He's a real jerk if I ever met one!"

Kenya held up her hand to shish London while she tried to leave another message in Storm's voice mail. It already was full making that task impossible. Kenya was heated throwing her phone against the still wet walls and pounding her fist on the table. London was startled and ran from the kitchen to see her sister enraged.

"I swear to God I'm gonna kill a motherfucker if something done happened to him!"

Just as Kenya finished ranting, Paris and O.T. pulled back up. London wasted no time in opening the door to let the pair in.

"Did you find out something?" Kenya rushed up to O.T. almost knocking him off his feet. "Did he call?"

"Naw Baby Girl." He hated to say. "But I did find out that nigga Royce's number and shit."

"Was he with them. Do he know something?"

"Kenya, pump ya' brakes will ya?" O.T. said moving her to the side so that Paris could get all the way inside. "His phone goes straight to voice mail too."

"Damn!" yelled Kenya.

"Relax girl!" Paris spoke up hugging her friend.

"When you and your sister get settled, I'm gonna shoot by Royce's peoples and try to find out if they heard from him yet. Just try to chill." He reasoned.

"I'm trying to be calm, but this whole thing don't make fucking sense!" Kenya shrieked.

"Listen up. Me and Paris done handled Deacon for now, but I still don't think it's safe in here. Yall should jet until we hear something."

"No kidding Sherlock." London interrupted.

The tension and dislike she was feeling for O.T. was transparent and obvious to the entire room. Being a career class 'A' ass hole was second nature to O.T. so he was used to people having an instant hatred of him. He finished his statement without even missing a beat.

"I'll fall through tomorrow and really clean up with bleach and some of that strong ass industrial strength disinfectant that's down at the club."

Everyone agreed with O.T. that it would be for the best for them to vacate the premises for the time being. Paris started to help London gather some of Kenya's things, so she and O.T. could take them to get a hotel room until they could get some workmen over to survey and repair the damaged condo. Besides it was no way on God's green earth that the twins were gonna spend one night in a spot where who knows what had taken place.

◎

"Come on yall got enough stuff for a few days."
"All right O.T. we're coming." Kenya replied.
After close to a hour of being in the house all four of them emerged out onto the porch. O.T. carried most of the bags to Kenya's car, while Paris grabbed the rest. London stood over towards the far side as Kenya locked up. In the mist of all the commotion the overflowing of the flower designed mail box was overlooked.

"Hey Kenya, it looks as if you've got a lot of mail piled up in this box. You want me to get it?"
"Yeah London. Just throw that mess in your bag. It ain't probably shit but bills and catalogues. I ain't got time to give a fuck about that junk now!"

Kenya double-checked the locks on the condo door. The same locks that failed to keep the intruders out.

London stuffed all the mail, including a small sized manila envelope, in her purse without even a second thought. She didn't take notice that the small parcel had nothing written on it front or back. Meaning that more than likely, someone had to have left it in the mailbox personally.

◙

After both taking showers, trying to unpack a few things and relax, Kenya laid across the bed dialing Storm's number once more, while London emptied the items in her purse on the dresser in search of a comb and a brush.

"Oh snap! What was that?" She leaped backwards.

"What's wrong London?"

"There's something moving in this envelope."

"What envelope?"

"This one." London pointed from a far.

"Where did you get it from?"

"Stop playing with me! It's the mail from your house! That's where I got it from!"

"Well who is it addressed to?" Kenya bit her lower lip as they both move over closer to the hotel door.

"Bzzzzzzzz." The envelope vibrated again.

"Go over there London and see what it is."

"Excuse me Miss Kenya, but that's your dang gone package, not mine!"

"Okay, but come with me."

As they slowly approached the dresser it buzzed once more. Kenya reached over carefully picking it up with two fingers and walked over to the lamp on the desk. She tried holding it up to the light, but couldn't make out its contents.

"Just open it." London insisted. "If it was a bomb or some junk like that we'd already be dead."

"Okay, okay, okay!" Kenya tore open the envelope dumping what was inside onto the bed.

"A cell phone and a ring box?" London casually asked. "Who would send you stuff like that?"

Kenya placed her hand over her mouth to muffle her scream. "That's Storm's cell phone! He's the only one that I know that has a neon green antenna on his shit and an airbrushed tiger on the back!"

"Are you sure?"

"Yeah! I'm certain." Kenya snatched the phone off the bed flipping it open. It said the words 'Capacity Full' across the screen.

"What about the box Kenya? Have you seen it before or what?"

"I'm still bugging out on this phone?" Kenya told her twin holding it up in her hand.

"Well, I'm gonna open it." London leaned over swooping up the small velvet box, shaking it slightly before peeking inside.

"What's in there?" Kenya waited.

"Ugh…..!" London dropped the box on the carpet revealing a note and a severed piece of an earlobe with a diamond earring attached. The same earring that Deacon was wearing. The same one that Kenya also owned. It was Storm's. That was proof positive that Storm was hurt bad, in danger or worst than that dead.

Kenya fell to the floor passing out. London didn't know what else to so she rushed to the telephone dialing the number that O.T. left. It was no need calling the cops they couldn't help anyhow.

YOU OWE ME

O.T. found the girl's together down in the corner near the door of the hotel room.

"Where is it at?" He scanned the room with his eyes darting around.

"By the side of the bed." Kenya threw her hand in the direction of the small box.

O.T. bolted to the side of the bed bending down on one knee. London watched the cocky, perfect muscle ripped, sagged-jeans, baseball cap backwards wearing thug, turn into melted butter as he held the evidence of his brothers harm in his rough seemingly strong hands. London could now, for the first time since encountering O.T. somehow relate to his pain. He now was a human in her eyes instead of a beast.

O.T. let his guard down sobbing loudly.

"Please don't cry. We're gonna figure something out. I promise." London cradled him in her arms while her sister was throwing up in the bathroom. She had been in Dallas less than twenty-four hours and was already entangled in obstruction of justice and another murder. Including Swift, the hit man back home, that was two all together.

"I'm tight ummm…London." O.T. could barely remember her name with all the chaos that was going on. He wanted to call her Kenya, but he caught him self.

He stood up first, reaching his hand down to assist London to her feet. As he and her were face to face, O.T. leaned in close, moving London's hair out of her eyes. Her inexperience romantic heart was working overtime. She shut her eyes and waited for him to kiss her. Feeling his body get closer, she held her breath in anticipation.

"Listen London." He whispered. "We good right? You ain't gonna tell nobody about that little punk ass faggot crying bullshit are you?"

"What!" London was pissed and disappointed that all he was worried about was people knowing that he was normal and had normal reactions. Her sudden fascination with him had come to a halt. "Is that all you concerned with?"

Kenya came back into the room on the tale end of the conversation between them.

"What's going on in here?"

"Nothing Kenya." O.T. answered for both.

"Yeah nothing!" London agreed.

◉

'You Owe Me' and a phone number was written on the note.

"What does that mean?" Kenya rubbed both sweaty hands together.

"We gotta call this number and hopefully we can find out." O.T. pulled out his cell phone and dialed the mystery person. An older sounding man answered on the other end. It was a voice that wasn't familiar to O.T. at all.

"Yeah!" The guy repeated twice before he got a response. "I hope you're ready to listen?"

"This O.T., who this?" He finally blurted out.

"I'm asking the questions here young man not you."

"Who the fuck is this?" O.T. was losing his patience.

"Is that any way to address your elders?" The man also was growing seemingly frustrated of all the cat and mouse talk. "Didn't your project living, three part time job working, two different baby daddy having mother teach you any manners?

"What did you say? O.T. was thrown off his square.

"You heard perfectly well what I just said and believe me I'm not in the mood or accustomed to repetitious conversation!"

"Nigga, how you know shit about my Moms?"

"Trust me. I know everything about your entire family. From your sorry excuse for a father to your third cousin twice removed on your mother's side and by the way I don't like to use the term nigga!"

O.T. was outraged by the stranger's overly blatant disrespect. "Listen dude! Where the fuck is my brother? I swear to God if you…..?"

The man cut him off. "You swear to God what? Please refrain from making idol threats. I have come in the past not to appreciate them. Now if you don't mind, can we get to the business at hand youngster?"

O.T. was for the first time since the call was placed silent. He looked at Kenya and her sister, both sitting on the edge of the bed anxiously waiting to hear any news at all.

The man started with the answer to O.T.'s first question. "This is Javier and your brother, Storm is here with me. For the time being he is safe from harms way. If all goes as planned he will stay that way. You have my word."

"How can he be safe motherfucker? Ain't this a chunk of his damn ear and shit?"

"What did I just mention about your mouth young man? Any further outburst will cause me to bring this call to an end. Are we clear?"

"Yeah, we clear." A once again silent, O.T. sat still after being scolded.

"Now as I was saying. Storm is here with me and alive, for the time being. If you have possession of this number it is very safe to assume that you already have come in contact with your brother's business partner and friend, Deacon."

"Yeah, if that's what you wanna call it." O.T. was being sarcastic and bitter. "Man, that shit was foul as hell! How could yall do some old crazy stuff like that?"

"That's life in the game we all chose to play, now deal with it!" Javier chuckled. "Your brother and his twisted personal life has caused me and my various operations major financial strains."

"How so? He has never been short on a payment."

"Because of him, his ex-stripper girlfriend and her do good sister, my cash flow has been slowing down. That is not acceptable."

O.T. looked at the girls and frowned. He now knew that it was because of them that his big brother was in serious trouble.

"What's the deal man?" O.T. wanted to skip straight to the point. He wanted to know exactly what it would take to get Storm back safe and sound.

"London Roberts, his sister-in-law and her little group P.A.I.D, have been causing a few bumps in the road." Javier spoke calmly. "It was some confusion as to the identity of her and her twin Kenya at first, but that mystery has been solved. Swift found out the hard way, but it's always causality in war."

"What the hell is P.A.I.D? And who is Swift?" O.T. wondered, as he attentively kept his ear pressed to the telephone receiver. "I don't follow you!"

"Listen O.T., you have to ask your people any questions. They can fill you in. My main concern is my revenue and nothing more. By my calculations your brother owes me approximately $750,000 dollars in lost sales. Although it's true he never has been late on his own payments, he is being held responsible for his peoples actions."

"$750,000 dollars! Are you nuts? That shit just ain't right dude. What fucking people?"

"I guess that Storm's safe return doesn't mean that much to you." Javier still remained calm. "I'm sorry to have troubled you. I guess that this is goodbye!"

"No, No! Wait!" O.T. stuttered. "I'll get the money, but it's gonna take me some time."

"I'm aware of that. I'm a fair man, so I will give you thirty days to gather it."

"Javier, I'll call you as soon as I get it."

"No, there's no need in calling this number again. I'll get back in touch with you." He demanded. "Thirty days, no more."

And with that exchange Javier hung the phone up leaving O.T. to explain to Kenya and London.

"What did they say? Where is Storm? Is he hurt bad?" Kenya fired question after question.

"Thanks to you and this bitch here, we supposedly owe Javier $750 gees to get Storm home. If we pay the dough he'll let him fucking free." O.T. was pissed and made no excuses as he mean mugged London.

"What do you mean 750,000?" Kenya was left puzzled by O.T.'s comments. "And why the fuck you calling my sister a bitch?"

"What is P.A.I.D?" He asked, slamming his fist down on the night stand causing it to tilt over.

London and Kenya made eye contact with one another. It was apparent that Storm's sudden disappearance and Deacon's murder were all linked back to London's passion, People Against Illegal Drugs. The connection was all coming together.

"Damn Frick and Frack! Is one of yall hoes gonna answer my question?" O.T. was now on his feet towering over the girls. "And who is this nigga Swift?"

Kenya jumped up in his face. "Hold the fuck on motherfucker. Me or my sister ain't gonna be anymore bitches or hoes, that's first of all."

"What!" O.T. spit out wildly. "What you say?"

"You heard me nigga. I'm gonna explain and shit, but you not just about to come up here in our room and dog us out."

"Oh yeah! Is that right?" His nostrils flared and the veins in his neck were ready to burst.

"Yeah it's right O.T." Kenya suddenly pounced up and swung on him. "I know shit is real messed up right about now and we all upset and worried about Storm, but you got me all fucked up! You better act like you know nigga!" Her punch missed its mark.

O.T. admired Kenya's spunk and backed down to hear her explain. "All right then." He sat back in one of the chairs folding his arms. "I'm listening and please don't leave shit out."

London was preparing herself for all the fireworks that were about to jump. She knew that she was gonna be number one on O.T.'s shit list.

"Well, first off, P.A.I.D. is an organization that my sister and her friend Fatima started back east."

"And?" O.T. was growing impatience.

"Damn! Calm down and let me finish."

"Go ahead Kenya."

"Like I was saying. My sister and her room mate were up at school and got together with a few other students to form a kids against drugs sort of club." London jumped in and clarified what exactly it was.

"It's People Against Illegal Drugs, and FYI it is more than just a handful of my classmates, it's almost the entire campus of my University as well as several other schools." She had her chest stuck out as she bragged about the strength of the group.

"Can you please shut the fuck up London? You trying to make shit worst or what?" Kenya had to put her twin in her place. Even though London was busy trying to act all high and mighty, it was her bullshit that had Storm being held hostage.

"Yeah London! Shut the fuck up!" O.T. co-signed with Kenya as he waved her off with his hand. London did as she was told and let her sister finish speaking, but gave O.T. the finger.

"Anyhow, the organization kinda spread out here to the West Coast. I'm sure that's the group that Storm and Deacon were complaining about. You know what I'm talking about, don't you?"

O.T. was disgusted as he seared at London. "You mean to tell me that all along your damn sister has been fucking shit up for our pockets?"

Kenya hated to admit to him that he was right so she turned her back on him as she continued to explain.

"I didn't put two and two together until a few minutes ago my damn self." She glanced over at London while running her fingers through her hair. "Okay. What about this buster named Swift? What's his role in all of this? Is that your hoe-ass man?" O.T. directed his assault of questions to London.

"No he's the man that tried to kill us!" She shouted out loudly for the whole world to hear. "In our own home 'Mr. Know So Much'. He tried to kill us! And right about now I would rather be back in Detroit and take my chances with another lunatic murderer than be in this God forsaken town with you! He was probably one of your dope dealing cohorts anyway!"

London's boisterous outburst left O.T. and Kenya dumbfounded. It was the most words that O.T. heard come out her mouth all evening.

"Bitch is you crazy? Who the fuck is you…."

"Come on yall. We need to put all this petty junk on the back burner till we pony up on that loot and get Storm back." Kenya brought an abrupt end to the heated exchange. "It don't matter what the fuck happened, the main agenda is Storm. Fuck that dumb shit. Yall two can fight it out later. We ain't got time to waste, so let's see how much money we already have towards the 750 gee's." Kenya took a pen out her purse and grabbed the hotel stationary out the desk drawer.

Calculating the ticket money from the workers in the streets, including the dope that they had stashed in reserves and the dough that Kenya had retrieved from the house floor safe, they were still short.

Much to London and O.T.'s surprise, Kenya announced that she was holding close to a little over a hundred grand in cash. She also made it clear that when she went to the bank to her safe deposit box, she planned on pawning the jewelry that Storm always insisted that she kept there. Lumped together with the cash O.T. had from Alley Cats, they still came up also $300,000 short. They had to devise a scheme to come up on the balance.

Kenya gave her twin a dirty look. She had only, just several months earlier, given London $15,000 out the kindness of her heart, that she knew good and damn well that London was still holding on to and all her other savings for that matter. Here now, her identical twin sister sat on the edge of the bed, quiet as a church mouse, not even speaking up and volunteering to give the dough back to help free Storm. From that moment on things would never be the same between the two. In a last ditch attempt for London to jump in and have her sisters back, Kenya spoke out softly in fear of the response, if any. "I got some money coming in a week or so from the sale of my Grandmother's house that I can kick in." Kenya sighed. "I hope shit works out. I love Storm." London still remained hushed mouth, not offering her share of Gran's house, breaking Kenya's heart.

O.T. wrapped his arms around Kenya. "Don't worry. It will. A nigga like me got a few more irons in the fire. We'll get it!" He whispered in her ear. "I ain't gonna just let my brothers life go like that!"

London watched the exchange of embraces from the two of them and felt jealous. *"Kenya gets every cute guy she wants."* She wanted to run across the room and rip Kenya out O.T.'s arms and take her place. London knew Kenya like the back of her hand and knew that her twin wanted her to give up her share of the revenue from the sale of the house. Without a second thought, there was no way in hell that she was throwing her inheritance out the window on some low life drug dealer that she never had even met. *"How could she put me in that position to risk losing my tuition money? What nerve!"*

DA GRIND

The days that followed were consumed with argument after argument between the twins. Each one of them were on edge for different reasons. London missed being back on campus with all of her friends, while Kenya focused her entire mental and physical strength on getting her fiancee back home in one piece. London knew that her sister had an attitude with her about her reluctance to contribute to the 'Save Storm Fund', but so damn what.

"How long are you going to stump around this room and not speak to me?" London inquired. "You need to grow up and handle things more maturely."

"Excuse the fuck outta me! Some of us can't go through bullshit and just blow it off like you." Kenya cut her eyes rolling them to the top of her head. "I'm trying to pony up on this dough and get my Boo home, not that you give a fuck!"

After clearing her throat, London fired back. "I care about you, not him. You best believe, if it was you that needed my money or my help, I would be right there, jimmy on the spot. Haven't I proved that to you time after time?" At this point she was all up in Kenya's grill. "If my memory serves me correct, wasn't I the one who just helped your funny acting so called friends carry a dead corpse to the car while you were busy putting on one of your all to famous 'Drama Queen' roles?"

Kenya couldn't understand why her sister was being so callous, but didn't have the time to figure it out. It was only one thing on her mind, Storm. She finished getting dressed and left a disrespectful London in the hotel room to fuss by herself.

O.T. had called earlier and wanted Kenya to meet him down at the club. When Kenya drove up she pulled into her parking space. As she stepped out the cool air-conditioned truck and into the sweltering Dallas heat, Kenya looked over to the empty space next to hers labeled 'Reserved.' *"Don't worry Baby. I'm gonna bring ya ass home where you belong."* She thought as she got the door keys to Alley Cats out of her purse and cautiously approached the entrance.

Before she got a chance to unlock all the doors, O.T. skirted up in the lot doing at least 80mph. He had the music blasting as usual. Straight foolin'. Kenya was spooked by him burning rubber and almost took a shit in her panties. "What's wrong wit ya crazy ass nigga?," were the first words that flew out her mouth when he got out his ride.

O.T. ran over to a heated Kenya, picking her up off her feet and swinging her around. "I got some good news for you."

"What is it? What is it?" She smiled temporary forgetting about his idiotic actions. "Did you talk to Storm? Is he okay?"

"Naw Kenya, I haven't heard from him." He put her down. "But I got us some more loot, plus a line on a good ass hustle that might push us over the top on that hoe ass buster, Javier's ticket.

Kenya was visibly disappointed that O.T. hadn't gotten anymore news about his brother, yet coming up with some more money would eased the load.

They both entered the club after disarming the alarm and got down to business. He informed Kenya that he was gonna set up a meeting in the club on Friday. He explained that he could double up on some good dope that he'd gotten a line on and possibly make all the money they needed. Kenya took her notebook out so that they could add up the new figures. O.T. took $35,000 out a shoe box that was behind the bar on the shelf and tossed it to Kenya. "Here you go."

Kenya reached for the stack of money that was crispy and smelt new. "Where did you get this from?" She questioned. "I hope ya behind didn't do what I think you did! Please tell me you didn't!" "Dig dis here. Don't be so damn quick to always think the worse about me." He paused as he checked his brother's woman and opened up a beer. After two long gulps, he eased Kenya's mind answering her question. "Ya girl Paris emptied out her bank account. You know she's down on my team!"

Kenya sat back on the bar stool, letting out a long drawn out sigh. She couldn't believe that her best friend Paris would kick in all her savings, while her own flesh and blood twin could care less.

"Paris always is there when I need her. You better treat her right boy! She deserves that!" Kenya pointed her finger at O.T. trying extra hard to reinforce her words. "I ain't playing with you either Negro. You need to make it legal like me and Storm is gonna do as soon as he gets home, get married."

O.T. guzzled down the rest of the beer in the bottle and twisted the top off another. "Please Kenya, you know I'm a damn Pimp!" He grabbed his manhood and chuckled loudly. "Matter of fact, where is that phat ass big mouth twin sister of yours at? Why she ain't roll with you? I got something for her!"

Kenya got up putting the money in her bag. With her keys in her hand heading towards the door, she laughed. "Okay Playa Playa. You best to stick with Paris. She's the only one that will put up with your foul behavior. And as for London, I think, naw let me re-phrase that, I know that she is a little bit out ya reach. My sister don't even get down like that!" They both gave one another the evil eye.

Kenya was pissed with London, but that still didn't stop her from chin checking O.T. "Go home to your woman with ya ignorant ass and I'll see you Friday!"

O.T. was left standing in the club alone and started reminiscing about him, Deacon and Storm playing pool and talking shit. O.T. poured him self a shot of Yak and agonized the near future. He knew that sooner or later he would have to end up making up some sort of a lie to Deacon's only family. It was only a matter of time before that 'he's on a vacation' bullshit would play out. How would he explain to Deacon's church going, bible toting, Grandma that her only grandson was murdered, beheaded no less.

The rest of the day, O.T. sat in the back booth of the empty, dark deserted club getting pissy drunk, smoking blunts and thinking about Deacon's body, that was buried in a shallow grave in the back of an abandon warehouse, as a worried Paris blew up his cell phone.

HOW DARE YOU

It was early Friday evening and Alley Cats was on bump. Everyone had turned out for the clubs most popular day, Freak Out Fridays, which meant a lobster, crab and shrimp buffet dinner along with a bottle of Moet with each time a customer got a dance from a girl in the V.I.P. room. They always had a couple more bouncers on duty on the weekends, for all the extra crowd that would pack in.

Paris and Kenya were out shopping one day and came up with the idea as a promotional gimmick to ensure they got the guys to stop in the club and spend a portion of their paychecks with them before they took the rest home to their wives and kids.

O.T. was busy posted behind the bar, giving one of his constant power drunk speeches to Dawson, the head bartender, on watering down the drinks in order to save a few dollars. Even though he knew that Storm or Deacon didn't believed in short changing the customers on drinks, dances or dinner.

Paris was occupied with collecting the house fee from the dancers before they stepped on stage and made their rounds of hustling the guys for tips. Staying on top of the girls was always Kenya's job, but she was running late, causing Paris to fill in for her.

With the clipboard in hand she checked off the names as they paid. Passion, Too Sweet, Addiction, Fatal Beauty, Tight-N-Right, Temptation, Sugar, Lil Bit, Lexus and Chocolate Bunny's nasty, big booty, trifling, always on the verge of getting fired for breaking the club rules, had all taken care of their business and were already on the grind roaming the floor getting that money.

◎

"Will you hurry up London? I've gotta get down to the club. We already late as a fuck." Kenya knocked at the bathroom door three times in an attempt to get her sister to rush things up. "Now come on! And stop all that bullshitting around!"

London was usually the one that was on time, but this was special. She was gonna see O.T. for the first time since that horrible night they met. London couldn't take her mind off of him. She kept Kenya up the night before asking question after question. Even though London tried playing it off, her twin was vibin' with her and could see right through her game. Kenya didn't have to twist London's arm one bit into going to work with her at the strip club. Especially when she found out O.T. was gonna be on the premises.

Paris was Kenya's best friend and it was no way on God's green earth that she was going to be apart of causing her even a moments worth of pain. If that meant cock blocking her sister, then so be it.

After ten more minutes passed, London exited the bathroom with a brand new bounce in her step and a huge grin plastered on her face.

"I don't know what in the fuck ya slick ass is so happy about. Storm is still out there somewhere hurt and you all hee-hee-ha-ha." Kenya announced. "You act like you don't even care!"

"What, it's against the law to smile in Dallas until your man comes home?" London returned her sister's sarcasm. "Well excuse me!"

"Listen here Ms. Thang! I guess you have over looked one damn thing, well let me remind you. O.T. already has a Wifey… Paris." Kenya placed both hands on her hips and bucked her eyes. "So if you have any designs on him, you better forget about it and keep it moving. We clear? Understand?"

"Whatever Kenya! I don't know what you're talking about. I don't like that low-life rude thug. That's more your style."

"Yeah right! Whatever my ass! Just don't forget what I said." Kenya pushed London's arm.

The twin sisters finally left the hotel in route to Alley Cats. It was sure to be one hellava long night.

◉

"Hey Kenya, how are…?" Boz the head of security couldn't believe his what he was seeing. He had the same reaction as O.T. and Paris.

"Close your mouth Boz before something flies in it."

"But…" He was stunned.

"I know silly. This is my twin sister London. Do me a favor and let her in the office through the back door and oh, please don't mention her being here to anyone. Not to the other bouncers, the dancers or anybody else on the staff."

Boz's eyes were glued to London as he walked with her around to the back. He noticed that although she was indeed a mirror image of Kenya's face, their mannerisms were outrageously miles different. Kenya walked like a panther seductively on the prowl for the weak, while London took each step with pride and confidence.

London noticed his strange expression. "Is there something wrong? Do I have a glob of snot hanging from my nose or what?" She winked.

"Oh my bad. I didn't know the bosses girl had a twin that's all." Boz laughed it off showing his mouth full of gold plated teeth.

Going inside the strip clubs doors and up the stairs, London caught a brief glance at the stage. One of the dancers was hanging upside down from the brass pole while others were sitting back wards in men's laps grinding, simulating sexual acts. When settled down on the couch in the plush office, her mind began to wonder and she felt sadden. London realized that only a short time ago, her sister Kenya was one of these females.

◉

"Hey Paris. How are things going so far?" Kenya found her friend in the dressing room going over some of the house rules for a new dancer named Jordan that grew up around the way from Paris. "Hey Woman! I was just thinking about where the heck ya crazy ass was at."

"Girl, you know I'm traveling with a little extra baggage." Kenya replied referring to her sister. "Oh yeah Kenya, dig that."

"How's things going?"

Paris finished up schooling the rookie on the do's and don'ts and went into the hallway followed by Kenya. "Everything's, everything. We got a full house already and it isn't even eight yet."

"That's what's up!" Kenya nodded. "We need all the cheddar that we can scramble up on."

Paris gave her girl a hug that was cut short by one of the dancers, Chocolate Bunny, who was walking fast yelling out to one of the bouncers. Her demeanor was louder and more ghetto than normal. It was obvious by the way she was waving her hands around and bopping her from side to side, someone had gotten on her bad side, which was almost impossible to do since Chocolate Bunny had an 'anything goes policy' a/k/a 'Fuck U Pay Me.'

"Excuse me Paris. Let me see what in the hell is gonna on with that dirty black skank. You know she always got some drama gonna on!"

Paris was glad that Kenya was finally there. If it was one chick in the entire club that she despised, it was Chocolate Bunny. It was no secret to Paris or any other person that worked in Alley Cats, that O.T. had fucked around with her back in the day.

Every chance that Chocolate Bunny got to get close to O.T. she took advantage of. Paris wanted to kick her ass on several occasions and had to be physically held back. She often lobbied for Storm or Deacon to fire Chocolate Bunny's slime ball behind, but she was one of Alley Cats main attractions and made a lot of dough for the club. That meant that Paris had too suck it up, like it or leave it and be a big girl.

◉

"What's the deal? What's wrong?" Pretending to be sympathetic, Kenya placed her hand on the dancer's shoulder. "Calm down and tell me!"

"Hey Kenya!" Chocolate Bunny looked at her. "It's that old ass wanna be pimp that yall had us chillin' with before. He must be nuts!"

"Nicole, slow down. Who are you talking about?"

"Are you fucking crazy Kenya! Don't be using my motherfucking government name in this bitch!"

If it had been any other circumstance that went down and a dancer, especially Chocolate Bunny, had screamed on Kenya like that, money maker or not, the bitch would hit the bricks. Kenya knew better than to use someone's real name in the club. A lot of perverts and stalkers sat around nursing their drinks in hopes of finding out where the girl of their dreams lived at and getting a dancer's legal name would be that gateway. Kenya didn't mind taking a cop.

"Damn chick, I'm sorry. It slipped." Kenya wasn't fronting, she truly was. "I fucked up."

Chocolate Bunny twisted her lip to the side pulling her dingy g-string out the crack of her ass. She knew that Kenya was rolling with Paris and would like nothing better than to see her dead or hurt. "Yeah all right! And to answer your question, I'm talking about that non-tipping ancient ass hole Royce!"

"Royce! Royce is in here? Are you sure? Where is he at?" Kenya scanned the room.

"Damn, yeah Kenya, I'm sure!" She pointed towards the rear of the club. "He's over there with his crew, talking about he is about to buy Alley Cats and trying to get free dances. You know a hoe like me don't play that crap no matter who a nigga is!"

Before Chocolate Bunny could finish her statement, Kenya had abruptly walked away, leaving her standing alone with the bouncer. *"Oh my God! Maybe Royce knows something about Storm. They was supposed to all be together when they left."*

Kenya spotted Royce dressed in one of his 1975 Mack Daddy suits and several of his friends seated in the corner just as Chocolate Bunny said. They had a few bottles of champagne and were surrounded by dancers.

"Excuse me Royce. How you doing?"

"Well, well, well. If it isn't Ms. Tastey."

"Pardon me." Kenya assumed, without doubt, that she must have been hearing Royce incorrectly.

Royce licked his lips. "Ah Tastey, Baby Doll don't be like that! With your pretty self."

"What did you say?" Kenya felt her world shatter once again. What Royce had just said was hard to digest. No one in Dallas, outside of Storm, O.T. and Deacon knew her as 'Tastey', not even Paris.

"Come on now Sweetness. There's no reason to be shy with Daddy." Royce rubbed her hand. "I'll give you double if you give me one of ya special dances."

"I'm sorry. I don't dance. I came over here to ask you a question if you don't mind." Kenya tried her best to keep her fronts up.

Royce pulled out a thick knot of money wrapped in a red rubber band. "You sure you don't want to come out of retirement and make this loot?"

"Listen Royce." Kenya was trying her best to remain professional as all eyes were glued on her. "I just need to ask you something in private."

"Why do you have a wire on you? Did the FEDS send you to fuck with me?" He stood up from the table. Everyone within ear range was quiet waiting for Kenya to respond. "Tsk, tsk tsk, there's no need trying to act naive young lady. I already know that you play for the other team. You snitchin' lil tramp! I saw the picture. We all did!" Royce raised his eyebrow. "Storm tried denying it, but we all knew."

"What the hell are you incinerating? Storm knew what?" Kenya's violent streak was surfacing quickly. She had came to him respectfully, in peace, in hopes of some info on Storm. Now he was calling her out. "Yall girls can leave. He's on his way out the door."

Kenya's teeth were clenched tightly and her lips trembled as she summoned the dancers to move on to another customer. They did as they were told in a slow fashion trying to linger around for the shit to hit the fan. "Hurry the fuck up before I start sending hoes home!" That threat made them speed up.

"Now back to you old man! How dare you insult me!" She lashed out. "All I wanted to know is if you know anything about Storm or Deacon? Why are you in here playing games with me! This shit ain't no joke!" Her voice was increasing with every word.

An angry Royce responded. "Pay attention lil whore! I don't know shit about that coward Deacon or Storm…ask Javier!" He stroked his unshaven salt and pepper beard, while straighten out his muti-colored polyester suit. His boys were all young in age, yet must have been inspired by their leader when they selected their gear for the evening, all looking like Royce clones. They were hanging on every word that slipped out his jaws.

"Matter of fact, here's a better suggestion for you.

"Why don't you ask the coroner at the local morgue?" Royce boldly suggested enjoying growing tension that filled the room. "Yeah, get in touch with them. They probably could answer all your questions better than anyone else. After all Tastey, Kenya, London or whatever name you're going by tonight, that is where snitches and bitches end up ain't it?"

Kenya straight was bugging out and shivering. She was completely drained from worry and was sleep deprived. Her body temperature was close to reaching boiling level from him exposing her private life to everyone in Alley Cats.

Royce and his friends were enjoying the sight of Kenya's high and mighty stuck up ass being brought down a couple of notches. They were still holding their glasses in their hands and smiling. She couldn't hold it together any longer. *"These busters think I'm here to entertain them. Yeah all right!"*

Kenya's mind was racing. Her palms were itching to smack Royce's ass. She used her finger to twirl her engagement ring as only one thought monopolized her brain, Storm coming home alive. Now Royce was putting shit in the game, making a scene.

"The morgue! What? The morgue! Did I hear you act like you know something about my man?"

"You heard what I said little girl!" He raised his glass as if he was making a toast. "Now get the fuck away from me before I kick your period on!" The crowd was amused by Royce's brazen words.

Kenya was hysterical. 5,4,3,2,1 Blast the hell off. Before Royce knew what was happening, Kenya socked him dead in his left eye. Followed by several combinations of right and left hooks, he was thrown off balance falling back into the booth knocking all the bottles of champagne onto the club floor. Her attack caught his smug crew off guard as they watched Kenya pounce on top of Royce like a sick deranged mountain lion. "Motherfucker, you done earned this!" She shouted with each blow.

By the time one of them could snatch her off of their boss and get him back on his feet, his face was scratched to the white meat, his lip was bleeding and his dentures were hanging out his mouth.

Showing no signs of letting up, Kenya wasn't done yet as she struggled to break free and continue showing Royce, who was boss in that motherfucker. "Let me go! Let me go!" Kenya's piercing screams could be heard throughout the whole club. "I'm gonna kill you slut, just like Javier killed that no good snitchin' ass man of yours!" He boasted. Royce's words were vindictive and sliced into her soul. "They can bury you both together in a cheap wooden box!"

Kenya broke free of the guy's grip just as O.T. and the bouncers approached them. She stole on Royce once again, this time tagging the other eye. Her nails had broken off into his face causing him to scream out like a little baby.

"Don't fold now nigga! I ain't done. Let's do this!"

"Yall better get that wild lil whore!," Royce tried commanding his boys, "Before I kill her up in here."

Kenya was on the zigitty nut boom and close to practically foaming at the mouth as Boz grabbed her up in his chest. With Kenya's legs kicking wildly and arms still swinging, Boz caught some serious hell in dragging her up the staircase to the office door. He had easier times trying to throw a grown ass, six foot two, three hundred pound, drunk and disorderly man out of Alley Cats than he was having with his bosses girl.

"I'm gonna get you Royce! I swear to God, I'm gonna lullaby that old wrinkled ass for good one day!" Kenya was leaning over the railing yelling as an exhausted Boz still struggled. "I swear, just wait! You got that shit coming Royce! On my parents grave! That's ya' ass!"

"Don't fret Tastey." Royce was putting on a brave front for the club patrons. His ego was bruised, but he still continued to talk shit. "I'll see you in them streets real soon and when I do, oh my! I'll teach your pole-swinging ass a priceless lesson of a lifetime! One that you'll never ever forget!" Royce blew her a kiss and smiled in spite of the severe pain he was feeling. "I'll see you soon little girl!!"

"SAY U PROMISE!!!

YOU OLD SON OF A BITCH!!!

SAY U MOTHERFUCKING PROMISE!!!"

Kenya managed to shout recklessly across the crowded bar as Boz finally literally pried her fingers off the railing and threw her in the office onto the couch next to her terrified sister.

" Damn Kenya! What was that all about?"

Play Ya Position

Kenya confessed to London the real reason that she hadn't mention her very existence to her friends and employees. "It's simple. I know that you can't stand drugs or anything affiliated with them, so why would I even get your named mixed into this world that I'm calling home? I mean be serious London, I already knew that any hopes of you accepting Storm and his lifestyle was little to none."

"Regardless Kenya, we're sisters. You act like as if you're ashamed of me." London argued. "No matter how much foolish stuff you've been caught up in the middle of, I've never turned my back on you or even once thought about it."

"Yeah, you right London."

"I know I'm right. So there's no reason to be up in here feeling sorry for your self. Things are gonna work out. Now chill Kenya, before you have a total nervous breakdown."

Kenya let her body relax. Her heart was still racing from her confrontation with Royce. "Girl, I think I better. That old bastard gonna make me hurt him."

"I was watching on that security camera behind the desk." London smiled. "You are in some serious need of anger management. I'm telling you Kenya, you are a straight up nut case."

"I know. I think I picked up some of your bad habits."

London hugged her twin. "You wish!"

Much to Kenya's surprise, during the course of their conversation, London announced to her that after long consideration, reluctantly she had decided to at least return the $15,000 gift that her twin had blessed her with.

"Thank you Sis. I knew that you wasn't gonna just leave me hanging like that. You best believe, that I wouldn't even think about being an Indian Giver if it wasn't a dog gone emergency." Kenya was counting every penny, as a penny closer to Storm's release.

"Stop that kinda talk. I'll call my bank sometime tomorrow and get the money wired out here."

"Thanks London."

◉

Meantime O.T. was left to settle up and iron things out with a half-crazed wounded Royce. "Man, what the fuck did you say to piss her off like that?"

"What the hell you mean what did I say?" Royce quizzed hunching his shoulders, wiping the blood out the side of his swollen lip. "That silly once a month bleeding bitch just went bananas for no good reason at all! She needs to be fucking medicated!"

O.T. studied the faces of Royce's crew as they listened to their self proclaimed leader punk out. They along with several of the dancers and patrons were stricken with amazement, that after blowing all that old style wanna be gangster bullshit out his busted mouth, Royce was standing in O.T.'s face taking a cop.

"Damn Dogg! It's like that?" O.T. turned his fitted baseball cap backwards. He cracked his knuckles while slightly smirking. Beads of sweat were quickly forming on his forehead. "Please don't let me even imagine that your ass is truly gonna go out like this!" The bouncers were all posted, ready to attack. "What you talking about Youngblood? Where you going with this?" Royce was shaking in his burgundy and yellow two-toned Stacey Adams as his crew put some space in between him and O.T.

When the shit jumped and the fists started to fly Royce was gonna be on his own. This was one stump down that his old school ass had coming. He had no business coming up in Storm's club beefing with his girl, talking all that 'la-la-la' mess. He'd crossed the line on number one of the player's code of ethics. Now, for real, for real, flat the fuck out, it was on!

A bigger crowd gathered around the booth after the D.J. stopped spinning records. Most of the girls held their g-strings in their hands and had stopped giving private dances to witness Royce get put in his place. Even Chocolate Bunny's hard hustlin' behind was waiting and she wouldn't let the Pope slow her flow.

The whole town knew that O.T. was on lunatic status, a true legendary mad man when it came to clowning. He was a few seconds shy of putting on a real show, a show so worthy that the streets would be buzzing about it for months and months to follow.

"Well, what's it gonna be Royce? You plan on being a man and pulling your panties out ya ass or what?"

"Come on now O.T., sit down and have a drink with me. Can't we handle this misunderstanding like two gentlemen? Player to Player? Pimp to Pimp?" Royce was trying his hardest to talk his way out of the situation at hand.

O.T. had blood in his eyes as he spoke. "Listen here Pops, I wanna work with ya, but I ain't gonna be able to." He frowned as his cheekbone twitched and he posted up. "The question is still on the table. You gonna have some balls and fess up or what? Trust me Royce! This is the final time a nigga like me gonna ask! You think Kenya whooped that ass, you ain't seen shit yet!"

"Okay, okay, okay!" Royce pleaded throwing his hands up in hopes of buying a few more seconds, stalling a beat down. "Pump ya brakes O.T., let me explain, but I guarantee you want to hear what I have to say in private. Please man, for old time sake?" Royce begged relentlessly.

"Yeah okay. I'm gonna hear you out and this shit better be good!" O.T. collared Royce up by his over sized lapels. "We can talk over there at my private table. Ya hoe ass boys can wait here!"

Royce was passed embarrassed, but still tried to save face and delegate some authority with O.T.'s huge hands firmly wrapped around his throat. "Yall dudes can chill over here. I'll be back."

His crew, like everyone else in Alley Cats had to laugh. Not only had Kenya and O.T. made a fool of him, now he was doing it to himself. It was official Royce was a Class A Idiot.

◎

After nearly an entire hour of listening to Royce talk, O.T. was heated. He couldn't believe what he was hearing. Royce was right. This was the type of information that shouldn't be made public.

"Come on now Royce, how many people you done repeated this story to? And try your best not to motherfucking lie!"

"To be honest with you, only my boys over there know about it." He nodded in their direction. "I've already told them to keep it close to the vest."

"Damn Royce! Good looking out." O.T. was playing the game. He wasn't dumb. He knew good and God damn well that if Royce hadn't already told the entire town of Dallas, he was well on his way. After all, If he or Storm had that type of dirt on Royce, you best believe that all bets would've been off.

"No problem Youngblood. We in this here game as Us against the Man. We gotta stick together."

O.T. was fed up with Royce's ass kissing, but he was glad that he'd heard what really went down with his brother, Deacon and Javier on the island.

From the pictures of London Roberts, one of the co-founders of P.A.I.D, being passed around the table to Storm's initial shock of seeing them realizing that his woman was playing both sides to the middle. Royce failed to mention to O.T. that he was the first one to put his brother on blast. He didn't want to risk getting beat down again, so he conveniently left that part out of the story. (Wouldn't You?)

Royce went on to explain how Javier had both Storm and Deacon physically removed from the round table and that he heard a lot of hollering and commotion from inside the Villa as he and the others were dismissed for the day. "I even tried reasoning with Javier, telling him that your brother wasn't like that and it had to be some sort of a mistake, but Javier wasn't trying to hear it." Royce threw in the conversation. "The next thing I can recall was two days later, Javier summoned us all back to the round table and dropped some knowledge on us."

Royce reached for a napkin to wipe the still slow dripping blood off his lip that was continuing to throb. "As I was saying, Javeir informed us that the Hit Man, Swift, that was sent out to Detroit to assassinate London Roberts, had himself been murdered." Royce paused to catch his breath. "Apparently not only is your brother's woman a straight up crazed bitch living a double life, she's hooked up somehow with a radical group in Detroit that calls themselves 'The Midtown Muslim Mafia.' They must be powerful as hell with they shit, because one of their members who goes by the name, Bro. Rasul had Swift's body shipped C.O.D to Javeir's front door with a note attached to his torso."

Mentioning the Detroit based hard hitters that Kenya and London were mixed up with caused O.T. to be silent as he listened to Royce's deadly tale of what could possibly have been his big brother, Storm's last days on Earth.

Royce could see the look of worry on O.T.'s face and decided to play his act for all that it was worth. He knew that he had to do a lot of fast talking and expert acting to convince O.T. to let him walk out of Alley Cats in one piece. Royce kept it coming. "I don't know what exactly were the contents of the letter, word for word, but I do know that Javeir stated that a horrible mistake had been made and asked us all to vacate the island by night fall. He generously gave us each a half a kilo of his finest product uncut, having us to swear to keep the situation under wraps until further notice. That's it!" Royce grabbed for another napkin trying to absorb the pouring sweat mixed with blood from his aging face. "No more was brought up about Deacon or Storm's whereabouts and who was I to question that man? A few hours later we were all put on a private jet and flown back to the States."

"Just like that?" O.T. sat amazed at the wild tale.

"Sorry I couldn't have given you more encouraging news about Storm's well being, but from where I stood, it didn't seem to pretty. But Javeir is very calculated about every move he makes, so don't give up hope. Anything is possible."

O.T. chose not to drop his hand letting Royce's back stabbing ass in on the fact that he'd already been in contact with Javeir and if things went as planned Storm would soon be home. Bottom line, you never let the left know what the right is doing.

O.T. signaled to Boz to escort Royce and his crew to the door. Before leaving O.T. made sure to make it perfectly clear that he was interested in buying some of that high quality dope that Royce was sitting on. Royce quickly agreed, knowing that if he didn't, it would more than likely be an all out open drug war in the streets of Dallas. His hands were tied tight.

Royce was a true Business Man and it was to his benefit to make money not mayhem. He really could care less where the drugs were being sold at as long as he got his money. What did he care, as far as he knew Storm and Deacon were both dead.

O.T. was a hot head and extremely arrogant about his shit, vowing to die first before letting other crews violate the blocks that him or his big brother ran. A nigga would be signing their own death warrant if they ever tried. He didn't give a shit about it being only two or three burn bags that a dopefiend was trying to get off, O.T. always kept it 'Gangsta'.

Those blocks belonged to them, point blank, period, end of fucking story! You feel me! Case Closed!

PAID IN FULL

London and Kenya left Alley Cats that night, staying secluded in the confines of the hotel until the repairmen had the condo back in livable conditions. O.T. delivered the profits from each night at the club and the loot that he made from other ventures. He made sure to flirt with London on every occasion he saw her. Kenya noticed an increasing change in her sister's behavior. London was acting sassy.

On the day the girls returned, Kenya was a bit worried her home, that people once described as a masterpiece, would not be repaired properly.

When the girls originally crossed the threshold of the door, Kenya took a long whiff trying to see if she could smell the scent of death in the air. She rubbed her cheek trying to figure out the difference between fresh paint and plaster and the everlasting imaginary stink of Deacon's lifeless corpse.

Taking a tour around her home, inspecting the workmanship, left Kenya having flashbacks of her and Storm's once perfect life. The stainless steel sink was clean and the kitchen cabinets were all freshly varnished. New appliances lined the walls. The floors had custom made marble that reached clear out to the patio deck. With the brand new living room set, along with the rest of the other overpriced furniture she charged, Kenya was somewhat at peace.

It was bad enough that Kenya had to live with the feeling of being violated, by strangers being in her private sanctuary, but she had no intentions of keeping not one stick of butter they might have touched. Even though some of the condo contents could be salvaged, Kenya wasn't interested. She wanted no reminders of their trespassing presence.

"Is everything okay?" London watched as her twin slowly made her survey.

"Yeah I'm tight." Kenya sighed. "I was just thinking about the days that we have left to hustle up on the funds we need." It was eleven days and counting and they were still short by $58,000.

◉

Although Storm preached repeatedly, time and time again to his baby brother, about hanging out, chillin' in the dope spots and actually making hand to hand transactions, at that point it didn't matter. O.T. stayed in the streets slinging dope, night after night, sun up to sun down… he hustled.

Paris was missing him, especially at night, but she had her own task, holding Alley Cats down. She had drink specials running all night long, even letting the fattest, ugliest girl's shake their asses on the big money making days. As long as a chick could come up on the house fee, which was raised to a hundred dollars a night, they were good to go. Everyone was doing their part, whether they knew it or not.

Paris' patience as Club Manager was being put to the test on a daily basis by the increasingly arrogant actions of Chocolate Bunny who hoe hopped around Alley Cats as if she owned the motherfucker.

Lately whenever O.T. came into the club, Paris would find him tucked away in some corner of the bar whispering in Chocolate Bunny's big floppy ears. (smile) As far as Paris was concerned, she wanted her man to barely speak to the chicks that danced there, then keep that shit moving. Breaking the rules to Chocolate Bunny weren't by accident, they were more like a force of habit. Paris held her tongue for the good of Storm's safe return. Yet, she knew in the back of her mind as soon as he returned home her claws would come out she was gonna wax the floor with Chocolate Bunny's face.

◎

Back home in Detroit, the real estate agent had contacted the twins informing them that there was some sort of hold up in the transferring of the deed to Gran's house and there would be a thirty to forty five day delay in the closing process. Any thoughts of relying on that dough, to push them pass their goal were ceased. It seemed as if that house was cursed.

Just as Kenya put her hand around the brass plated banister to go upstairs her cell phone rang. "Hello."

"As-Salaam Alaikum, Kenya. Is this you?"

"Bro. Rasul! Bro.Rasul!" Kenya was elated as she smiled from ear to ear. "I'm so glad to hear from you. I wanted to get in touch with you ever since we got back in Dallas, but I knew better."

"Al Hamd li Allah." Bro.Rasul added to his greeting.

"Praise be to Allah." Kenya repeated to him.

London ran to her sister's side. "Is that your friend? Is Fatima with him?" She grabbed for the phone. "Can I speak to her?"

Bro.Rasul heard all the questions. "Tell her that Fatima is back up at the University and sends her very best wishes. She wanted to call London, but I also explained to her that it would be best to lay low until I got to the bottom of all of this."

London was close enough to the cell phone to hear what the man that had saved their lives said. She believed in him for some strange reason. After all, Bro.Rasul did put his own safety and freedom on the line for them and for that he forever earned her trust and respect.

"I'm glad that you did as I told you and waited for me to get in touch with you." He praised her.

"So much chaos has happened since we got here. We came home to find, Deacon, my fiancee's partner dead in my house and some crazy son of a bitch is holding Storm hostage until we …"

"Until you come up with $750,000." Bro.Rasul finished a shocked Kenya's sentence. "I heard."

"Who told you? How did you find out?"

"Whoa, slow down little sister. I told you I was gonna investigate the situation and I did just that."

"Oh my God! Oh my God! Did you find out any information about Storm? Is he okay? Did you speak to him?" Kenya sobbed, shaking from nervousness.

"Yes and no." A calm voiced Bro.Rasul went over his conversation that just had taken place, less than a hour ago, between him and Javeir. "It seems as if your friend's host, turned kidnapper, was first infuriated at the actions of Fatima and London. Apparently their wide spread organization P.A.I.D caused a lot of financial downfalls for quite a few slimy low life drug dealers infesting the neighbor hoods and killing our greatest resource, kids. The marches on drug houses caused many to shut down."

"Oh, I see." Kenya interjected feeling ashamed that Storm was one of the drug dealers that Bro.Rasul was referring to. But never the less, she still wanted him home safe and sound. The world be damned.

"Well Kenya, after sending one of his henchmen, Swift, to Detroit to execute this London Roberts person, he some how came to find out that Storm had been dating her. It seems as if Javeir and everyone that was in attendance at this meeting, who saw the pictures for the first time being passed around, assumed it was you, Kenya A/K/A London Roberts. Do you understand what I'm saying?"

Kenya's mind flashed back to the altercation that she had in Alley Cats. It didn't take a brain surgeon to figure the whole thing out. Kenya couldn't avoid the truth any longer even if she wanted to. This was concrete evidence that Bro.Rasul had gotten straight from the horse's mouth and it was crystal clear.

"Now it made sense what Royce meant when he called me a snitchin ass bitch. That's why he called me London. Oh fuck! He must have seen the pictures and thought that she was working with the police. I mean

he thought that I was. Damn!" She started to hyperventilate and wheeze when it hit her. The two worlds Kenya systematically did her best to keep apart, were now colliding. Then the next alarm rang in her head. *"Oh shit! If Royce's ass saw those pictures, then I know that Storm must've seen them to. Oh my God! I can't believe this! I know he must be going out his mind. My Baby probably thinks that I betrayed him. He must hate me right about now! Why didn't I just be honest and tell him from the git go?"*

London took the cell out her panicked sister's hand. "Hey now, this is London."

"Hello London. Where is Kenya? What happened?" London glanced over at a blank faced looking Kenya and answered Bro.Rasul's question.

"I'm sorry, but you should know how she is by now. You know Kenya over reacts with everything she says and does. She's playing the Drama Queen."

"Come on London. That's your sister. You have to realize that she's going through a difficult and trying time in her life now. So give her a break." Bro.Rasul was acting as both peacemaker and therapist.

London listened to Bro.Rasul's speech with growing anger almost wanting to throw up. The feeling of animosity towards Kenya and the whole mess was fueling her out burst. "I know she's catching it right now, not knowing if Storm is alive or not, but what about me? Who's feeling any sympathy for my plight!" London was visibly enraged. "I should be back at school with Fatima working on my degree, not stuck here playing Inspector Gadget!"

For the first time since being in Dallas, London was determined to make someone hear and understand her point of view. Playing the back round was over. It was her time to vent. She went on and on, not giving Bro.Rasul a second to get a word in edge wise.

As London was almost out of breath from all of her screaming, O.T. entered the room. She saw him coming out the corner of her eye and decided to pour it on extra thick. "No one loves or cares about me! What about me?" She sobbed out loud, as the fake tears flowed, dropping the cell phone to the carpeted floor. "Who's going to look out for me and my future? I'm scared too!"

O.T. reached down picking up the phone and yanking London into his body in one quick motion. "What's wrong? What's the deal Baby Girl?" O.T. wrapped his arms around London's waist. "Tell me."

London continued to play the weak role as O.T. spoke to the person on the other end of the phone. "Yeah Hello! Hello!" He was eager for a response as he kept a clinging calculating London in his arms. "Peace. Whom am I speaking to?" Bro.Rasul remained as always, even toned.

"This is O.T. who this?"

"My name is Bro.Rasul Hakim Akbar. I am a close friend of the girls."

O.T. loosen his grip on London realizing who he was speaking to and the power the Royce mentioned that this man held. "Bro.Rasul. I've heard of you."

"I in trust that it was all positive and uplifting, but in all fairness I must admit that I don't know you." Bro.Rasul was respectful, yet guarded as he spoke to this stranger. He had no intentions of socializing with just anyone. "Can you please let me speak back to one of the twins? We have a bit of unfinished business that I need to inform them of."

"No problem dude, but first I need to know if you know anything about my brother's whereabouts?"

"And just who is your brother?"

"His name is Tony Christian, but he goes by the name Storm. He's Kenya's man! I know you've heard of him!" O.T. was tired of all the formalities. "Look, I already know you down with them 'Midtown Muslim Mafia' cats! I know yall bodied that nigga Swift that tried to do Kenya and London."

O.T. rubbed his hands across London's wet face and drew her back close to him. "Tell him I'm straight London. Tell him it's all good."

London leaned her cheek next to O.T.'s "Hey Bro.Rasul. This is Storm's brother. He's been helping us and making sure that we stay safe." London made sure to mimic Kenya trying to look sexy and seductive. She softly bit the side of her lip just as Kenya often did to get her way with a man.

"Okay then little one, I'll tell him what I wanted to put Kenya up on." Bro.Rasul agreed.

O.T. was all ears. "All right guy. You heard her, now tell me what you know about my brother. Is he still alive or what? What's the real deal?"

"Well, I just got off the phone with Javier. He told me that he gave your family thirty days to come up with $750,000."

"Yeah, that's right," O.T. huffed, "and that's some bullshit! Straight up extortion!"

"I know. That price is a little steep even if Javeir feels like he's been wronged somehow."

"Wronged how! Storm didn't know shit about all that P.A.I.D. crap." O.T. walked to the other side of the room away from London. "How is he to blame?"

Bro.Rasul could feel O.T.'s intense fury over the phone. "Listen O.T., I'm not calling to discuss who's right or who's wrong or who owes who what. My organization tries not to get involved in the drug game. That's not our main objective. We have other concerns." Bro.Rasul finally dropped the bomb, putting O.T. out his misery. "I just wanted to let

Kenya know that I settled up the rest of the debt that Javeir was strong arming you all out of."

"What does that mean dude? Cut all the cloak and dagger out!" O.T. was confused and wanted some answers in plain English, straight to the point.

"What it means is Javeir has given me his word as a gentleman, that in less than forty eight hours, your brother Storm will be released and returned home."

"Are you for real? Don't be fucking around with my emotions!" O.T. blurted into the phone causing Kenya to shake off her self-induced pity party trance and run to O.T., pushing London aside.

"Javier reassured me. He knows that we don't take pleasure in being lied to." Bro.Rasul snarled. "I know that you are overjoyed O.T., but slow down, there's been some discomfort and pain that your brother has been made to suffer, so prepare yourself as well as Kenya."

"I know. That old crazy dude sliced part of my brother's earlobe off."

"No not that. I'm afraid that it's a little bit worse than what you think."

"How much worse?" O.T. hesitated asking.

"The damage had already been inflicted. It was nothing that I could have done or said to have prevented it. Just tell Kenya to remain strong and to call me if need be. Peace."

O.T. flipped closed the cell and led both girls into the living room sitting them both down on the couch.

"Well O.T., what did he say? Is Storm coming home? Has Javier changed his mind?" Kenya held onto his hand squeezing it extra tightly jumping back up.

"Sit back down Kenya and pay attention. This shit is deep."

"Yeah Kenya! Sit down!" London added watching O.T. like a hawk. "Let him finish!"

A bitter O.T. tried to the best of his ability to prepare Kenya for the unknown circumstances of Storms' arrival, even though he wasn't truly sure himself.

WHAT'S DONE IS DONE

"It's six hours short of the deadline that Bro.Rasul said." Kenya paced the floor. "I wonder should I call him and see what the problem is?"

"Naw Kenya, don't call him yet. He said Javier gave him his word, so let's just ride it out and see. We done waited this long, we can go another six."

"Okay O.T, but one second after six hours and I'm calling, flat out." Kenya's palms were sweaty as she wore a path in the carpet from the door to the window and the window to the couch.

London, Paris, Kenya and O.T. were all posted, congregated in the front room watching the wall clock move slowly. It was like shear torture for the group waiting and wondering what was Storm's physical and mental condition going to be. Kenya, having the most to lose, was on edge more than anyone else, in the house. Storm was her life.

As the clock ticked, the tension could be cut with a knife. You could almost hear a tiny pin drop if you listened carefully. It seemed as if every fifteen minutes the silence was broken by O.T.'s cell phone ringing. Even after turning it to vibrate it could still be heard in the midst of the quiet that surrounded the room. Each time he would look down at the screen and see the caller I.D., he got agitated.

Paris and his arguing increased a lot over the last few weeks, because she knew deep down in her heart, despite his denials, that he was up to no good. "I wish that disrespectful bitch of yours would stop blowing up the damn phone!" Paris blurted out with malice. "Don't she ever sleep? All day and all fucking night!" She went on. "Tell that cheap hoe to get a life!"

"I already done told your silly insecure ass that I ain't fucking around, so stop bugging." O.T. kissed Paris on her forehead as she pulled away. "Chill out crazy. Ain't nobody getting daddy's dick but you!"

"Whatever!" Paris didn't believe him one bit, just as London, who felt jealous and somehow betrayed. It was bad enough in her eyesight that he was claiming Paris as Wifey, but now she had some other non-educated loser as competition for his affections.

"Why is he doing this? He's knows I like him?"

London's mind went over and over the reason in her head a million times as she watched, envious of the couple's interactions. It was making her sick.

"Can yall all just shut the fuck up for a minute and put that stuff on the back burner? Yall making me even more nervous, shit!" Kenya halted the heated argument between the two, with rage in her voice.

"Yeah, can you two please be quiet?" London was quick to jump to her sister's defense, although she had secret motives. "As much as I hate to interrupt your altercation, this isn't the time or the place to discuss your intimate personal problems."

Everyone agreed as London turned the radio onto a jazz station, coaxing them to try to relax. She then disappeared into the kitchen to fix some coffee for the group. *"Maybe everyone will calm down."*

She put the kettle on the stove turning the fire on high. After getting some mugs out of the cabinets and rinsing them all out, London felt chills rush throughout her body as a pair of big strong hands firmly gripped her waist. She could feel the warmth of O.T.'s breath in her ear as he whispered. "Hey Sexy, what you in here doing all by yourself?"

London's legs were growing weak as she tried to speak. Turning her around with ease, O.T. pressed his tongue deep into London's mouth. His dick was hard as a rock as he shoved her up against the sink and started to grind. London was for the first time, feeling raw dog nasty ass passion.

Even though, thanks to the brutal rape she suffered at the hands of her devious Professor, meaning she was no longer a virgin, she still was unaware of what she was feeling. Her pussy seemed to have a voice of its own and was calling out to O.T. London was feeling an out of body experience. The fact that Paris and Kenya were only yards away in the next room only added to the thrill and shear excitement that the two were creating. The kettle was getting hotter.

◙

"I'm sorry about all that girl, but I know that nigga is back fooling around with Chocolate Bunny's behind. They always be exchanging funny looks and notes and shit. My home girl Jordan, from down at the club, said that black bitch has been going around bragging about some new buster that she done hooked up with." Paris seized the opportunity as soon as O.T. excused his self to go to the bathroom to fill Kenya in about her dilemma. "Jordan even told me that cum drunk Chocolate Bunny has been flashing a big ass motherfucking ring!"

"Shut the fuck up Paris! Don't play with me! I know that nigga ain't laying down with that tramp!" Kenya forgot, about her own problems, for a hot second and joined her friend in talking about O.T.'s known cheating ways. "That fool ain't done lost his mind! He's knows that ya ass will bounce!"

"He better not let me find out for sure cause if I do, I'm done, that's my word!" Paris relationship was in limbo and on the verge of ruin. She sat back quietly puzzled at where she went wrong with O.T. .

Kenya regretted the fact that her twin sister was attracted to O.T. and knew given the time or the right circumstance, the two would probably act on that emotion. She was shocked that Paris couldn't pick up on it. Her woman intuition radar must've been broken. Even Ray Charles could see the way they carried on. *"Oh Shit!"* Noticing O.T. was taking a long time returning from the bathroom, Kenya jumped to her feet and ran into the kitchen.

◎

The kettle started to whistle a piercing sound as Kenya abruptly entered the kitchen.

"What the fuck are yall doing?" She jerked her sister and her best friend's man apart. "Have yall two lost yalls mind? I know you are both aware that Paris is right in there." Kenya pointed. "Why would you jeopardize getting caught and risk losing your woman? Is all this creeping shit wroth it?" Directing all her questions toward O.T. gave London a chance to remove the loud sounding kettle from the stove. "Dang Kenya, why don't you chill with all that talk. You must want us to get caught up and shit!" O.T.

put his index finger up to his lips and headed out the room. "I'll be in there with my baby, Paris."

Kenya was infuriated with London. That was the final straw. "Have you lost your damn mind? What the hell has gotten into your sneaky ass? This kinda crap don't make no freaking sense! Do I have to remind you that Paris is my damn friend?"

"No Kenya, you don't!" London was up in Kenya's face. "That's all the hell I've been hearing ever since I got here in Dallas. Paris this and Paris that. Well, I'm sick of it! So there! Fuck Paris and you!"

Kenya was thrown off by the fact that her sister was cursing and all up in her face as if she was ready to attack a bitch.

"Oh, it's like that now?" Kenya grinned braced to swing on her sister. "I guess you a big girl huh?"

"Yeah, it's just like that!" London refused to back down this time as the twins stood toe to toe. "So now what are you going to do Miss Drama Queen?"

Paris walked in the kitchen just in time to stop the girls from coming to blows. "Hey what's wrong in here? Yall act like yall about to throw down."

"Nothing." The twins answered at the same time. They put their family argument on hold as all three of the girls rejoined a smug faced O.T. in the living room. Kenya grew fed up and was about to explode. "You know what?" Kenya asked looking at Paris.

Before Paris got a chance to reply, there was a soft knock at the front door causing everyone to pause and stopping a frustrated Kenya from busting on O.T. and her sister.

Getting up, pulling his pistol out of his waistband and putting one up top, O.T. signaled. "All right Kenya, open up the door!"

◎

Kenya turned the knob on the door and cautiously pulled it open. She peaked out barely getting a glimpse of the tail end of a black Yukon driving off as quietly as it apparently had driven up. Kenya looked down receiving a happy, but sad sight. It was Storm laid out on the front porch. His back was turned, but Kenya could tell that it was without a doubt him. It was her Man and he was home. Now things could go back to normal.

"O.T., hurry up! It's Storm! He needs help!"

Paris and O.T. ran out onto the stairs leaving a hesitant London standing alone waiting to come face to face with the all so famous Storm. Even though she helped out in giving up her money for his safe return, she didn't know him, so it was hard for her to show genuine concern.

O.T. put his hand on his brother's shoulder and took his time carefully turning him over on his back. "That motherfucker!" O.T. mumbled with Javier on his mind. He was pissed to see his brother looking like he did. Paris covered her mouth in total disbelief, while Kenya's already fragile heart skipped a beat and crumbled at the sight of her once strong, handsome, devoted fiancee.
"How could they?" Kenya cried into her hands.

Storm's face had been mutilated. Not only was his earlobe sliced, his entire right side of his jaw was bigger than Kenya's hand. His lips were cracked and dry as if he hadn't had water or any other fluids in days. Storm's body weight was decreased by at least twenty pounds since Kenya and O.T. last saw him.

His left leg had a make shift kind of medical bandage attached to a splint. Storm was delirious and dazed. "Come on yall and help me get him inside." O.T. ordered. "We have to get him on the couch and off this hard cold concrete."

Paris let her anger with O.T. go, as she bent down positioning her self to help lift Storm. "Kenya, we need you to get on his other side so we won't bump his leg. Hurry up because I'm losing my grip." Standing frozen momentarily, Kenya snapped back to reality and took Storm's twisted leg in her arms. London could see that the trio was struggling so she rushed over, swinging the door open wide as she could, hoping to score points with O.T. for helping.

When they got a semi-conscious Storm on the couch, turning all the lights on brightly, they got a chance to fully take in the true harshness of the way that Storm was treated. Storm's eyes were rolling in the back of his head and he was mumbling words that made no sense to any of them. It was as if he was what the old people call 'speaking in tongues' or 'talking out the side of his head', like he was insane.

He was drifting in and out of conscious and wasn't aware of his surroundings or any of his family around him. Storm was fucked up bad!

"That fried bean eating motherfucker Javier is gonna pay for this! I don't give a shit how long it takes! Ain't nan son of a bitch alive walking this damn earth gonna do this type of bullshit to my family and live long to brag about it!" O.T. kicked the end table causing the lamp to wobble.

"Listen Baby." Paris caressed his back as she tried to soften his fury. "Now is not the time to trip. We should be thanking God that we didn't get Storm back in a body bag! Now we gotta call somebody and get your brother some medical attention. That's first on the agenda."

Remembering how Deacon made it home, London agreed with Paris as they stood on each side of O.T. watching Kenya on her knees kissing Storm's swollen face. "I'm so sorry baby." She repeated as she wet his split lip with a moist rag.

O.T. flipped open his phone and strolled down his locked in numbers. He went down a long list until he found it. "Here it is!" He announced happily. "Bernard Crayton." O.T. waited for the person to answer his call. "Hey dude, this is O.T., I need you to do me a solid. A.S.A.P., It's an emergency!"

◎

"From the looks of things, without the aid of x-rays it seems as if Storm's leg is broken. Now considering the swelling and the color tone of the bruises, I think it's healing, but if it isn't put in a cast and set properly, he might end up with a permanent limp."

Dr. Bernard S. Crayton had gotten to the condo in less than twenty minutes after O.T. placed the call to him. He was a regular fixture down at Alley Cats and on call 24/7 anytime one of the fellas would need him. He was a licensed Plastic Surgeon by trade, but treated everything from a hangnail on a cat to one of the hot box dancers at the club that was running around setting all the V.I.P. customers dicks on fire. Big Doc B, as everyone called him would write a bitch a prescription for having a bad hair day if she paid him enough. He was shady as a motherfucker, but knew his shit. "Let's move him to a bed and get him undressed so that I can examine him fully and get a better look at the damage."

As Kenya led the way, O.T. and Big Doc B carried the completely passed out Storm up to the bedroom. "Lay him here." She yanked back the covers and started undressing him as the guys talked over on the other side of the newly decorated master suite.

"You know that this shit is on the hush, hush right?" O.T. focused in on Big Doc B's eyes.

"Come on Pimp, how you gonna play me? You know me better than that." The doctor reassured him.

"My nigga!" O.T. smiled. "My nigga!"

◉

London and Paris were left standing alone downstairs once again. It was much like the night that the two had first met only this time the victim in the house was Storm instead of Deacon.

"I wonder what's going on up there? I hope he's all right." Paris put her hand on her chest. "I know Kenya is tripping out right about now."

"I know. I've been on my knees praying every night that Storm was safe." London was lying through her

teeth as she tried to befriend Paris. "I know that
O.T. is happy. Maybe now you two can stop all that
silly bickering and live happily ever after."

Paris went and plopped down in the chair, feeling
the brand new soft butter leather. "Naw London,
I'm afraid that it's a little bit deeper than just Storm
being gone."

"Dang gee Paris, I'm sorry to hear that." London
smirked behind Paris' back. "Do you want to talk
about it?"

"Nope, I'm tight. I ain't trying to start crying."

"Maybe you should just get it off your chest!"

"I don't want to bore you with me and O.T.'s
problems. I'll just have to deal with him and that
black spook Chocolate Bunny on my own."

"It's all right Paris. We're friends aren't we?"

"Yeah girl, but I'm gonna just sit here and think."

London was disappointed that Paris chose not to
confide in her, but she wasn't going to let that stop
the fake compassion from pouring. She wanted O.T.,
Thug or not! Paris' man or not! Fuck Chocolate
Bunny! Santa Claus! and The Tooth Fairy!

If Gran was watching down from Heaven, she would be ashamed at how London was behaving. Yet, London felt like the world had stepped on her for the last time. From day one she always tried doing the right thing and the only reward she got in return were several swift hard kicks in the ass. Life for London was not fair, it was fucked the hell up.

Her parents were both murdered. Gran was gone. Her favorite uncle, Stone was killed. Her virginity was taken from her against her will. She had to suddenly drop out of school and now the only thing or person that she had left to cling to, Kenya, was slowly being snatched away by these strangers that her twin now called family. It was no way that London intended on that happening, no matter what the cost. Her vindictive alter ego had taken over. *"What's taking them so long up there?"* London thought staring at the stairs. *"I hope that O.T. is okay. Maybe he needs me?"*

◉

Kenya had only gotten around to removing Storm's filthy sweat soaked shirt, when she noticed a huge gauze taped across his shoulder. When she pealed it back it revealed an ugly open sore. "O.T. my God! What is this? What happened?"

The doctor ran over and investigated. "It's looks like a gunshot wound to me. As far as I can tell, I think the bullet went in and out. I need to get a closer look at him. Hurry and flip him on his side."

O.T. did as he was instructed gently handling his older brother. He held him in his arms just as their mother use to do when they were kids. Big Doc B rubbed his hands over Storm's back.

"Here it is! Here's the exit wound. Yeah it was a clear shot, in and out." He verified his earlier prediction. "And it appears as if it has been treated with bacteria ointment of some sort. There's no signs of infections. Someone cleaned it up pretty good."

"What the hell does that mean? Is he okay?" Kenya worried. "Shouldn't we take him to the hospital?"

"We can't." O.T. cut her off. "That shit is out!"

"Yes Kenya, I'm afraid he's right, we can't do that. You see, the doctors are sworn by law to contact the authorities when treating any gunshot wounds." Big

Doc B reasoned with her. "Besides, like I said, all and all he's okay and healing just fine. Just let nature take its course. In the meantime, I'm gonna give you some morphine to keep him sedated and still. If he awakes in pain keep him calm and up the dosage slightly. I can also give you penicillin to fight off any of the remaining infections."

"How is he gonna eat?" Kenya inquired. "Or pee?"

"When he awakes, even for a few seconds, feed him warm broth, even if you pour a little bit down his throat, but the other part is on you. I sure hope that you're up to playing nurse mate for a couple of weeks. Storm's gonna need it!"

Kenya glanced back at Storm who was tossing and turning and seemed to be gasping for air.

The doctor had O.T. go out to his car and bring in a big sealed cardboard box. After they got Storm comfortable in the bed, Big Doc B opened the box and pulled out ointments, syringes, penicillin and plenty of morphine. He instructed Kenya in all the aspects of being the perfect caregiver to the badly injured Storm.

Storm was finally resting peacefully, back at home, in his own bed. With an I.V. in his arm, a slow drip morphine keeping him doped up and all his wounds treated, the doctor was finished for the night. O.T. escorted Big Doc B out to his car and paid him a nice chunk of change for the long extended house visit and his silence.

Kenya stayed next to Storm's bedside rubbing his forehead and begging for his forgiveness. Paris fixed some tea for them both and made her way upstairs, deciding to spend the night and lend her best friend some much needed moral support. That left O.T. and London all alone in a dimly lit living room.

"Is she okay up there?" London whined leaning her head on O.T. "You think Kenya needs me?" London would be first in line to receive an Academy Award for her acting performance. She was starting to care less and less about Kenya's feelings.

"Naw, I think I might need you. How about that?" O.T. had a long rough day. Seeing his big brother and hero broken down had taken a heavy toll on him. "Come to think of it I do need you." O.T. rested his head in London's lap and in no time flat he was snoring not once giving a second thought to Paris being in the same house.

"Things are about to be in my favor for once! O.T. said he needed me! Not Paris' stuck up ass and not that slut bag Chocolate Bunny, but me!"

London couldn't help but smile as she closed her eyes and finally dozed off to sleep. Hopefully, Paris and Kenya were upstairs doing the same. They had all had enough drama for the day and Paris catching her man cheating would only make the day end with a bang. No doubt about it, it was going to be a long couple of weeks for Kenya, Storm, Paris, O.T. and London.

Da Game Ain't Fair

Several days had passed and Storm was basically still out of his shit. There was little to no change in his overall condition. The swelling in his jaw was going down, but still had some bad bruising. The gunshot wound was the only thing that appeared to heal quickly. Storm would move his bad leg from time to time in his sleep, when he would scream out, like he was a small animal being hunted down, caught and killed. Watching him in that state made a weary Kenya cry on the regular at his bedside.

The perfect brush waves Storm always sported were gone. His hair was growing daily and nappy as a fuck. His beard was thick and looked down right messy as hell. And even though Kenya kept his face washed, his once brown perfectly toned skin was dry and blemished. With all the weight that he had dropped since Javier first held him hostage, Storm was only a shadow of the man that used to be. He stayed unconscious most of the time because of the intense pain he was suffering, making Kenya's job of getting even a tiny sip of soup down his throat almost an impossible task. And then it was keeping the covers dry and clean, which was a bitch, seeing how Storm was pissing on his self and sweating like a motherfucker. Kenya refused to use the Depends undergarments that Big Doc B suggested. She felt like that was humiliating for her fiancee to have to deal with when he did come back to reality.

When he would awaken, all Storm would do was moan and mumble about a lot of nothing. Each day seemed to stretch out longer and longer before he would fully recover to his old self and things got back to normal. Kenya was tired, but was devoted.

Big Doc B stopped by every other day to examine Storm and check on his healing process. Slowly he was decreasing the amount of morphine that Storm was under the influence of. He didn't want to keep him sedated so long that he wasn't able to regain use of his leg without the aid of therapy. Big Doc B knew that some of the excruciating pain, Storm would have to be a thoroughbred trooper and man the fuck up. It would be some hard shit to do, but nothing that Storm couldn't handle.

◎

KENYA

"I don't know how much more of this I can take."

Kenya was distraught and moving around like a dead zombie. Staying up late at night, waiting and catering to Storm's every need was breaking her down. She was starting to truly look like hot death on a stick. It had been days since she had a long hot bath or sat down to watch her stories on television. Her hair was standing on the top of her head and her face had forgotten what make up was. Every moment that Kenya was awake, she spent posted by Storm just in case he opened his eyes. London would help at times, but felt like it wasn't her duty or her responsibility to be a strangers slave. Only when O.T. was around would she put on a front and act like she gave a shit about Kenya or Storm.

Kenya had just finished changing the sheets and getting Storm settled when she heard her cell phone ring. She kissed Storm on his lips and went into the den to answer the call.

"Hello?"

"Hey Kenya! What's good woman?"

"Who is this?" Kenya yawned sitting back on the couch laying her head back on the arm.

"Oh it's like that? Ya ass out in Dallas and forgot about me and your Godson that quick!"

"Oh my God! Young Foy is that you?"

"Yeah it's me. I was just checking in with you and wanted to give ya sexy self some good news."

"I need some good news right about now. I hope that it's about Jaylin. Does he miss his Auntie Kenya?"

"You know he misses you, but that ain't the news."

"What is it boy! Stop playing with me!" Kenya managed to crack a smile for the first time in weeks.

"My C.D. just hit the shelves! That's what's really good!" Young Foy was excited and Kenya could feel his energy through the phone. "Me and Jaylin is gonna be rich. My shit is about to blow the fuck up."

"Damn, I'm so happy for you. I knew you could do that shit. I always told you that you had mad skills."

"Yeah, you always did encourage a brother and help me get on my feet. That's why you the first person that I called. I got love for you Kenya, flat out."

"I got love for you to. My girl Raven is probably up in heaven dancing on the clouds with pride."

"I miss the shit outta her ass. Jaylin is starting to look more and more like his Momma every single day that passes." Young Foy glanced over at his sleeping stepson and smiled. " I'm bout to head to the cemetery in a few and take some fresh flowers. I feel close to her when I'm there."

"Next time I'm back in Detroit, I'm gonna have to go out there." Kenya rested her eyes, momentarily reminiscing about the good old days when her and Raven were hustlin' hard making all the cheddar in Heads Up.

"Me and Jaylin both will be glad to see you."

Before the conversation ended Kenya's call waiting clicked in with another call. It was from Paris and O.T.'s crib and she had to take it.

"Hey that's my other line. I'm gonna call you back later on tonight and give Jaylin a huge hug and kiss from me."

"Okay Kenya! I'll holler!"

Young Foy hung up and Kenya answered the other line. "Hello?"

◙

PARIS

"Why every day it gotta be the same old fake shit from you O.T.?" Paris was in the bathroom yelling at O.T. as he took his morning shower. "You just got in this motherfucker at three thirty in the morning, now you back out the door again! Nigga I ain't slow or crazy. Ain't shit open that late at night, but the jailhouse and a stankin bitches pussy."

O.T. continued to let the hot water pound his body as he zoned Paris out his mind. His hands rubbed the soap on his chest and let his imagination drift to thoughts of fucking the shit out of London. He had his fingers up inside of her tight moist pussy and had sucked on her titties, but had never actually given her the dick. His thick long manhood throbbed from his hands letting the later work its way up and down as he stroked it hard. At that second O.T. would have spit in his dead great grand mothers face if he could have had London bent over with his dick knee deep up in her. He loved Paris as much as a man could love a woman, but her constant nagging was starting to turn him off. His motto was that there was nothing better than pussy, than brand new pussy. And London was his target.

"Do you hear me talking to your nickel slick ass?" Paris yanked back the shower curtain and rolled her eyes immediately catching a serious attitude. "I'm trying to talk to you and you in here beating your motherfucking meat! You ain't shit!"

"Why don't you get out of my ear with all that ying yanging and put your mouth to better use?" O.T.'s shit was about ready to explode, with or without Paris. "Now come on!"

"Nigga please. Why don't you get that bitch you was with last night to suck your little dick? That broken as cell phone of yours called me back after you hung up and I heard them bitches giggling and shit."

"Damn Paris, stop tripping and come get on your knees!" O.T. let what his woman said come in one ear and fly out the other. "You know ain't shit little about this motherfucking monster I got in my hands!"

Paris was pissed off even more, by O.T. ignoring the information, she'd just confronted him with. "Didn't you hear what I said, with your trick ass? I heard that slut talking about the ringer on her phone being Gold Digger!" Paris pulled her robe tight and folded her arms. "What kind of real woman would have that bullshit on their phone? Don't fuck around and give me AIDS or something! You're a poor excuse for a man!"

O.T. had enough of her accusations and insults. This time he was innocent and didn't feel like all that drama she was bringing. O.T. was pass running late for an appointment and still had to swing by a couple of his dope spots before he headed for his meeting. He was determined to get his nuts out the sand before he left and snatched an angry Paris into the shower with him. Her hair was now drenched and her short pink robe was soaking wet causing her nibbles to harden. In the middle of her struggling to break free from him, O.T.'s dick got harder than it ever had been before. He quickly turned her around pressing her face on the wet shower wall and raised up her robe. He ran his hands down the crack of her ass and soon he had his index finger working her out. Paris was out of breath and gave in to her man as the steam filled the bathroom. He shoved all nine and a half inches up into her while he watched the water drip on her backside. Right before he was about to cum, O.T. shut his eyes imagining that she was London. He tilted his head back and almost busted for what seemed like a hour straight pass eternity. "Now! Do that seem like a nigga been fucking around on your silly ass?" O.T. blew Paris a kiss as he stepped out the shower grabbing a towel to dry off. He splashed on some Armani Black Code and started getting dressed. Rubbing lotion on his face and brushing his hair, he double-checked the mirror twice, clipped his cell phone on his jeans and got his wallet out the nightstand. "I love you Paris!"

Paris was too exhausted from the beat down that he had just put on her to even argue. "Whatever!"

"Here's some dollars for you to go get your wig tightened up for Daddy! And buy a new outfit." O.T. pealed off four or five hundreds and tossed them on the dresser before he left out the door. "I'll be back later Boo! Keep it hot for a nigga!"

Paris was left speechless as she heard him pull out the driveway and away from the house.

"I know that bastard is cheating on me!"
She had to vent and decided to call her girl. Maybe she could convince her to go to the hair salon with her. After grabbing the cordless phone, she dialed Kenya's cell and waited for her to pick up.

◎

GIRLFRIENDS

"Hey Kenya. Are you busy?"

"Naw chick, not really. I was just taking a little break and just got off the phone with an old friend."

"Girl I'm sitting over here mad as a son of a bitch. If I didn't have a lot of self-control, I think I would put two bullets in O.T.'s cheating ass!" Paris stood in front of the mirror brushing her wet hair back into a ponytail.

"Slow down Paris." Kenya knew that her best friend was in pain and mentally tired of O.T. and his crap.

"Naw girl. Enough is enough. I done had it!"

"Paris. You ain't making any sense. Tell me what went on over there."

"First that fool had the nerve to slither his behind in the house at damn near four this morning." She argued. "Even when I close the club at night that nigga will bug out if I'm more than five minutes late, but he thinks he can fall up in the crib whenever!"

"Dang! Where did he say he was? Or did he?"

Kenya shook her head with disgust.

"You know that bullshit would be to much like right, but that ain't even the bad part!" Paris threw herself on the bed and put her feet up on the wall. "His cell phone dialed me back by mistake and I swear to God I heard that tack head Chocolate Bunny running her big mouth in the back round."

"You lying to me!" Kenya was now also frustrated about the shit. "Please tell me you lying Paris!"

"I wish the fuck I was. And when I asked the two timing dog he started playing the dumb role, then he had the audacity to flip the script and take the damn pussy!" Paris was shouting into the phone receiver by this time and was back on her feet. "If I didn't have an allergy to fucking prison, I'd kill him!"

Kenya couldn't understand why O.T. couldn't be loyal to one woman and was so damn ruthless. He was a bona fide hoe! If she was dealing with a Negro like that, it would be no way that she would tolerate all the mess that Paris put up with.

O.T. would stop by the condo every afternoon and sit by Storm. He filled him in on all the news from the club and the streets. The fact that Storm was doped up on morphine and didn't even realize that O.T. was in the room, never once stopped his brother from talking. O.T. had a split personality. He was like Dr. Jekel and Mr. Hyde. He was sweet as pie one minute and the next, a beast.

"Kenya, I ain't lying. That boy gonna end up in a casket one day double crossing a bitch like me!" Paris knocked a framed picture of him to the floor.

"Why don't you come over so we can kick it in person? I can get London to cook us up some hot wings and fries." Kenya suggested.

Paris looked at herself again in the mirror coming up with a better ideal. "Why don't I just swing by and swoop your ass? We can hit the Steak House, then the hair salon. How bout it?"

"Girl, you know I can't leave Storm."

"You need to get out and get some air. Your sister can stay home and look after him." Paris pleaded with her best friend. "I know you look a hot mess."

Kenya noticed that her three of her fingernails were in bad need of a fill in and her polish was chipped. She then tried running her hand through her hair, but was stopped by a few naps. "Yeah, I do need a touch up and a manicure."

"Then it's settled. Let me get dressed and I'll come get you!" Paris was geeked to have her road dogg back.

"Pump ya brakes Paris. I gotta go ask London first."

"Okay, but hurry up and call me back before I jump in the shower and wash O.T. off me."

"You silly as hell." Kenya laughed. "Give me a minute to check and see what's up."

Paris and Kenya automatically assumed that London would be the perfect person to stay with Storm, considering the fact that 'she didn't have a life of her own.' Kenya's life and world had somehow swallowed it whole. The best friends never thought that maybe London wanted to go out for lunch or get her hair done. She was also stuck in the house, in a strange town, with no friends at all. But that didn't stop Kenya from asking her anyway.

Kenya stopped in to check on Storm before going downstairs. He was quiet and seemed to be resting peacefully. Since the dosage was decreasing he seemed to be in and out of conscious more often. She kissed him softly and made her way to the lower level of the condo.

When she got in the living room, she found her twin sister doing something that she'd never seen her do before. London was stretched out across the couch, feet up on a pillow, watching rap videos and even acting like she was enjoying them.

"No you ain't! I thought you said videos were stupid and degrading to women? Now ya behind sitting up here posted like a motherfucker!"

"Shut up!" London threw a pillow at Kenya "I'm just looking at this ghetto trash trying to understand exactly what every one finds so interesting."

London was a lie and the truth wasn't in her. She had been keeping her eyes glued on the way the girls danced and moved their asses, to the way they dressed. She understood why O.T. liked Paris, who was smart, pretty and always had his back. Paris truly had her shit together, that part was undeniable.

But that serpent Chocolate Bunny was all together different. From what London had heard about her, she was no more than a dirty un-kept gutter rat. Whatever O.T. saw in her, Paris, Kenya and London were all hard pressed to realize. Maybe all the wild nasty videos would shed some light on the dilemma and help London to turn O.T. on. If it took being sleazy and a little hot in the ass to achieve the ultimate goal of having O.T. all to herself, then so be it, that's what she'd do.

"Listen London. Would you mind sitting upstairs with Storm for a few hours so I can run out for a little while with Paris? Please?"

London had been hoping and wishing that Kenya would leave the house so that she could be alone with O.T. when he would come over for one of his daily visits. Now was her time and to make shit even better, Kenya was hanging out with Paris. She would have O.T. all to her self.

"Yeah, I'll stay here. No problem."

Kenya went and called Paris back informing her that shit was a go. She took a quick bath and got dressed. London stayed downstairs and plotted her seduction game plan. Twenty minutes later Paris pulled up and blew her horn.

"Don't worry about Storm. I'll make sure to check in on him every fifteen minutes and give him his medicine on time." London convinced her sister. "Go and have a nice time. He's in good hands."

"Say U Promise!" Kenya hugged London.

"Yeah, I Promise!" London walked her twin to the front porch waving 'Hello' to Paris.

FUCK DA WORLD

O.T.

O.T. had the sounds in his car on bump causing all the other car windows to vibrate that he passed along the way. The long valet line at the Mall's main entrance didn't matter one bit to him as pulled up to the front and parked his ride up on the curb. Him and his brother not only knew the parking attendants, they hung out with the owners on a regular basis, making O.T. feel like he was above waiting for shit. He threw the guy his keys in case of emergency and walked inside.

He was already ten minutes late and wasted no time in going over to the designated meeting spot over near the food court. It was always busy with people moving about, so him and his visitor would more than likely go un-noticed. It was no way that he wanted to draw attention to them. He looked around and didn't see the person yet, so he decided to order a large soda. By the time he reached in his pocket to pay the cashier for it, she was there.

"Hey Babe. Did you get me something wet to put in my mouth?" She flirted while sticking out her tongue to reveal the small gold ball pierced through the middle.

"Damn girl! You slick with your shit. I didn't even see your ass coming." O.T. ordered her a small soda to drink and fought the urge for her to lick the head of his dick just like she used to. "A brother better be careful dealing with your good creeping ass!"

"You know how I do Baby. Ain't shit changed since back in the day." She sipped her drink slowly out the straw as staring into O.T.'s eyes.

"I heard that!," He took a large gulp of the soda and tossed it into one of the garbage cans, "but I'm trying to take care of some other shit today so I need to hurry the fuck up!"

O.T. took his time as he scanned the room for signs of any trouble or un-welcomed eyes on them. When he felt the coast was clear he pulled out a gigantic knot of money, big enough to choke King Kong and slipped it casually into Nicole's over sized purse.

"Do I need to count it?" She playfully teased pushing his arm. "Or can I trust you?"

"Act like you know! I don't make moves that ain't right or have you forgot?" O.T.'s eyes shot down towards to the huge print in his pants. "I'll expect to hear from ya smart ass tonight!"

"Yeah, yeah, yeah, I'll see you later at the club, don't worry." Nicole grinned, closing her purse. She stood up, straightening out the ultra short bright red sun-dress that was plastered to her thick frame.

"That's a bet, and be on time!" O.T. winked, getting a quick glimpse of her two firm breast which were close to almost falling out of her clothes.

"Damn, I almost forgot. Can you keep a secret?" She put one hand on her hip and the other in his face.

"What is it?" He waited for her to answer. Nicole leaned up and whispered in O.T.'s ear causing him to smile. He then hugged her tightly and kissed her on her forehead before they parted ways. "Drinks on me later." O.T. insisted as he walked away to valet.

◎

"Ain't that some foul ass shit?"

Paris' home girl and spy down at Alley Cats, Jordan, happened to be at the Mall at the right time. She was busy spending the money that she made from doing a private party the night before and fucked around and got an eye full of what was sure to be labeled 'the gossip of the year.' Paris' man O.T. was giving Nicole Daniels a gang of loot. After all the denying that he was doing to Paris about that tramp, he was out in public, in the middle of the freaking food court no less, tearing the bitch off and to top it all, hugging her black ass.

"Hell Naw! I've gotta call Paris!" Jordan smirked as she whipped out her cell to put O.T. straight on blaze. *"It's gonna be a whole lot of crazy shit jumping off at Alley Cats tonight."* Jordan thought to herself as Paris voice mail clicked on. She left her a message.

"Hey girl, this is Jordan. Hit me back as soon as you get this. I need to put a bug in your ear about a little something. Trust me you're gonna bug all the way when I tell you what I just seen."

◉

GIRLFRIENDS

"Kenya, I'm so happy that you came out to hang with me." Paris had the air condition on high and a mix C.D, pumping. "I miss ya crazy ass!"

"Me to. You know I love Storm like a motherfucker, but a bitch did need some air. Plus look at my nails and please let's not even mention this tangled mess on my head! I walked pass the mirror this morning and scared the shit out of myself."

Paris and Kenya couldn't help but laugh until tears came out their eyes. It was just like old times. "What about this crap?" Paris snatched one of O.T.'s baseball caps off her head. "If that nasty fool nigga wasn't so busy trying to take that pussy, my shit wouldn't be on the nut."

They had just finished up with lunch and were on their way to the hair salon. *Hair In Da Hood* was the most popular spot in all of Dallas when it came to getting your hair looking top notch. It stayed packed with wall to wall customers that would often range from lawyers and doctors to freaks and hoes.

Charday was the salon owner and the main stylist that everyone wanted to do their shit. Her chair stayed full. Most of the time a person would have to make an appointment at least two or three weeks ahead of time. But of course Ms. Charday would always make exceptions for her special clients and her good friends. And since Paris and Kenya where known for being big ass spenders when it came to tipping, they automatically fit into both categories.

Her man played professional ball and bought *Hair In Da Hood* as a birthday present for her 21st birthday. After some major remodeling and a gang of commercials, Charday was off and running in the hair game, clocking major figures.

Nine out of ten times, even if you got there early, you'd end up leaving late. In between the bootleg movie guys hustling, some bodies grandmother selling soul food dinners and all the off the wall gossip that would fly in, out and around the salon, it could very easily turn into an all day event. Some of the nosey bitches around town would live for the weekends so they could get into the next hoes mix.

Never the less Paris and Kenya were on a mission to pamper themselves for the day and that meant no stress and no drama or trauma.

"I've got a good idea. For the rest of the afternoon, let's make a pact not to bring up, mention, whine or complain about that pair of brothers." Paris stuck her hand out and waited. "Well, you gonna leave me hanging or what?"

"Naw chick, I got you!" Kenya gave her a play.

"Now that's what the fuck I'm talking about!" Paris yelled out as she adjusted the volume up as high as it could go.

The girls put their seats back as they floated down the road towards the salon. Fifteen minutes later they were pulling up in a crowded parking lot, trying to find a space.

"Damn! Is every trick in town up in that joint?" Paris frowned as she pulled her car into a tiny corner of the lot. "I hope our girl ain't booked. I'd hate to have to smack somebody out the chair, but my shit is on emergency status." Paris looked at Kenya with a straight face like she was serious.

She turned the car off and reached for her purse that was on the back seat before she made her exit. "Dang, you right Paris." Kenya joined in on talking shit as she got out the car. "Charday and them must be giving away free cheese and butter inside. I ain't never seen this motherfucker on bump like this either."

The girls swung the door open and stepped inside. Just as they figured, the salon was packed. Sable, was the receptionist and was standing behind the desk trying her best to reason with one of the many irate customers that were getting tired of waiting.

"Hey yall!" Sable waved up her hand. "Long time no see. Where yall been hiding?"

"Just chillin a lil bit, that's all." Kenya replied.

"Yeah Sable. We call our self letting our hair have a break from all the chemicals." Paris added trying to play off their recent absence from the scene.

"I heard that." Sable responded seeming frustrated at the phone that was ringing non-stop and the angry woman with conditioner in her wet hair that kept coming back up to the desk to complain.

Kenya took a quick survey of the room and asked the million-dollar question. "Hey Sable, how many chicks do Charday have backed up in this tiny motherfucker and can she squeeze us in?"

"Well, let me check the book. I'm sure she can work something out." Sable grabbed the sign in sheet and took the pencil out from behind her ear.

The lady who was standing there was pissed and sucked her teeth as she waited for Sable's answer. She had been there ever since 8:45 in the morning and still hadn't been rinsed or blow dried. Once again as always, Charday had over booked.

"I'm gonna go speak to Charday myself." Kenya stopped Sable from rearranging things. "I'll be right back."

Paris twisted her lip up at the lady and let out a loud sigh. "Go ahead girl and see what's popping. I'll wait here and keep Ms. Thang and Sable company."

The woman took that as her cue to go back to her seat, shut the fuck up and wait until she was called. It was either that or nine out of ten times get a quick double trouble ass beat down from Kenya and Paris.

When Kenya returned she had good news and bad news. The good news was that Charday could fit them both in, but they had to give her at least thirty minutes to finish up with the girl in her chair. The bad news was that she had to slip Charday a crispy hundred-dollar bill and promised her a bottle of new perfume for the deed. It was all part of being Storm and O.T.'s girls. They had to play the role, after all no matter where they went, bitches hated. It came along with the territory being labeled 'The Shit.'

Paris and Kenya sat down next to the angry woman who had pulled out a book and was totally engulfed in reading. She appeared not to even care anymore, that she was still waiting as she turned page after page without once looking up.

Kenya noticed the title of the novel and the hot slamming cover. *"Get It How Ya Live."* She repeated to herself. *"I gotta remember to grab that shit the next time I call the bookstore."* Kenya was more and more getting into reading. Ever since the first night that she started dancing she was a weekly customer at *Hood Book Headquarters*, back home in Detroit.

Now that Kenya was living in Dallas the chick that owned the store would send her the latest releases. Kenya made a mental note to herself about the book as Paris got comfortable.

Paris opened her purse and got out her cell phone to look at the time. "Shit, I didn't hear this thing ringing." The screen said 'two missed calls' and had a small envelope in the upper corner indicating that someone had left a voice message. Paris stepped into the bathroom to listen to the message. It was much quieter in there. It was no women gossiping and the sound of the loud radio and television was muffled. *"Jordan wants me to call her as soon as possible. What the fuck could this be about?"* Paris wondered as she returned the call. On the first ring Jordan picked up.

"Hey Paris, what took you so long?"

"I had my phone in my purse, what's the deal?"

"Before I tell you this bullshit, you'd better sit down first."

"Stop tripping and tell me! What's going on?"

"Well girl, I was just out at the mall jacking off some spare change and guess who the fuck I saw?"

"Who?" Paris heart started pumping fast as she awaited the answer from Jordan. From the tone of Jordan's voice, Paris could tell that the name that was sure to come out of her mouth would bring automatic fury.

"I seen that hoe Nicole."

"Nicole! Who the fuck is Nicole?"

"You know who I'm talking about…Chocolate Bunny, that damn Nicole!"

"And? What's the big deal about that? Hoes gotta shop to!" Paris tried to crack a joke to ease the pain of what was coming next.

Jordan didn't laugh as she gave her home girl the low down. "Yeah, but she wasn't alone. She was at the food court all hugged up with O.T."

"What!" Paris closed her eyes. "Are you for sure?"

"Yes Paris, I'm certain." Jordan reassured her of what she had just witnessed. "He was wearing some dark colored jeans, a Pistons jersey and Tims. That trick Chocolate Bunny had on a skin tight dress and was rocking a big Gucci Bag. Knowing her fake ass it was probably bootleg!" Jordan added.

"It's all good in the hood. I'm gonna handle it."
Paris pretended to be brave as her hand shook.

" Oh yeah, I even saw him give that slut a nice size knot of loot! I wanted to follow her and rob her my fucking self! With her stanking no good ass!"

"All right Jordan. Good looking on the info. I'll see you tonight at the club."

Paris was heated as well as devastated. She went inside of one of the stalls and shut the door. When the tears started to flow she didn't want any of the women in the salon to see her at one of her weakest moments. After ten minutes of having an emotional fit, she splashed cold water on her face went to fill Kenya in on the latest.

◙

"What took you so long in there?" Kenya inquired.
"I was on the phone."
"Talking to who? And why are your eyes all red and shit? Have you been crying?"

Paris pulled her hat down over her face in an attempt to shield any nosey bitches from noticing the same thing that Kenya had. "I called Jordan back. She left me an urgent message."

"What kind of message? Is everything going all right down at Alley Cats?" Kenya hoped that shit was in order. She didn't have the time or strength to go to the club and straighten out a damn thang.

Paris was agitated as she tried her best whisper. "It ain't the club. It's O.T.'s no good ass. Jordan just seen him at the fucking mall."

"What's wrong with that?"

"He was there with Chocolate Bunny." Paris felt like she had just been socked in the stomach as soon as the words passed her lips. "All up on the bitch!"

Kenya was almost speechless. "Is she sure? You know how females like to start rumors."

"Girl she knew exactly what that Negro was wearing, from foot to fro." Paris sniffed her nose. "The worst part is, his ass is serving that black bitch up like a queen. Jordan said he gave Chocolate Bunny some dough like she was Wifey."

"That nigga must be smoking!" Kenya said with her hand on Paris' shoulder. "Something ain't right!"

Less than ten minutes passed in between the time that the best friends tried to figure out what was wrong with O.T. for doing that dumb shit and the five seconds it took Chocolate Bunny to come through the door of the salon. She was dressed just the way that Jordan explained. All the way down to her purse, which by the way was bootleg.

She marched up to the reception desk like she owned the bitch. "Yeah, I need Charday to tighten up my weave real quick!"

"I'm sorry Nicole, but she's all booked up for the rest of today." Sable chewed her bubble gum and gave her a funny look. "What about tomorrow?"

Chocolate Bunny reached in her handbag and started flashing money. "I'll pay a hundred dollars to any of yall that wanna give up yalls spot with Charday!"

While she was show boating, Kenya was trying everything in her power to keep Paris in her seat. "No that chick ain't up in here spending my money. I outta go over there and knock her ass out!" Paris was fuming. "I hate the fuck out of her!"

"Listen Paris. It is what it is! Don't let that girl or any other of these females up in here, catch you off your square! Do you hear me!?" Kenya was all up in Paris ear being the voice of reason. "Now come on and let's just jet before you embarrass yourself. We can deal with her later. Besides you should at least give O.T. a chance to explain before you mess around and hurt somebody. Go call him!"

Paris finally agreed. When the pair was almost out the door, Chocolate Bunny spotted them and decided to make a scene. "Hey ladies! I didn't see yall sitting over there. You two could have spoken." She was being fake as a three-dollar bill. She knew that it wasn't no loved shared. The only thing that they had up to this point in common was Alley Cats.

"Hey girl." Kenya nodded. "We kinda in a rush."

"Okay then, don't let me stop you." Chocolate Bunny laughed. "Or you either Miss Paris!"

Paris couldn't take it any longer. Her temper was on boiling status. "Listen up bitch don't even speak to my fine ass! A hoe like you ain't even in my damn league! Now carry your messy behind the fuck on, before I give your family some arrangements to make for ya!"

"Who you calling bitch!? Is you insane!?" Chocolate Bunny sucked her teeth looking Paris up and down. "Don't be threatening me either Paris, I don't like that kinda shit! Me or my Man!"

"Yeah right! You got me all fucked up! I don't make threats I make promises!" Paris pointed her finger in her face. "Fuck you and him! Believe that!"

Kenya stepped in the middle before either one got a chance to swing. The entire salon was staring at the group. Charday came over and asked them to calm down or leave. They were all good clients, but business was business and they were all tripping.

Before Paris and Kenya could get out the door good, they heard the song Gold Digger playing. It was the ring tone that was on Chocolate Bunny's cell phone. Paris had a flashback of the other night when O.T.'s phone dialed her back and sucker punched her in her jaw causing her to fall to the floor.

"She was pass due on that one!" Paris snickered as her and Kenya finally got in the car and pulled off.

HOW COULD YOU?

O.T.

Driving down the interstate with the warm air blowing on his face, O.T. let the music take control of his mind. He was once again lost in thoughts of London's perfectly shaped ass. He secretly always wanted to fuck the shit out of Kenya, but considering the fact that she was Storm's woman, that made her off limits. Seeing how London was her identical twin, she was the next best thing to actually sticking the dick to his brothers' girl. In his mind it would be like hittin' them both off at the same time.

As O.T. felt his hard pipe through his jeans, he smiled seeing his exit and quickly made the turn. It was now only a couple of short blocks to get to his brother's crib for his daily visit. His dick was stiff as a board. If he played his cards right, O.T. hoped he might get a few minutes alone with London, at least to feel on her titties.

Kenya always did her best to cock block him when it came to her sister, letting him know that it was no way that she was being apart of any back stabbing conspiracy plotted against Paris. If London was in a room with O.T., you betta best believe that Kenya was in that bitch to. Day after day Kenya informed him that wasn't a damn thing going down on her watch. Little did Kenya or O.T. have any ideal that today would be his lucky day.

◎

LONDON

No sooner than Kenya and Paris bent the corner, London ran back in the house and straight up the stairs. She tipped toed into her sister's room, pass a sleeping Storm and went into the closet. It was now time to select an outfit that would make O.T. lose his mind when he saw her. For days, she had taken notes from the videos and knew that with Kenya out the house, she might finally have the chance to put her plan in effect. After snatching a short blue jean mini skirt off the hanger and a powder blue T-shirt that was sure to fit tight, London headed for the shower.

She used some of her sister's favorite cucumber melon body wash as she felt the warm water hit her nude body. London then rubbed in plenty of the matching lotion after drying off.

Slipping on Kenya's new shell covered sandals she pranced down stairs. She then admired her work in the mirror. London now looked exactly just like Kenya. Her once dull appearance was gone. The bait was set for O.T. to get trapped.

"I know that he's gonna want me now! If this doesn't entice him, I don't know what will." She thought as she hugged herself. *"I just hope that he gets here at the usual time and Kenya stays gone. I don't need any obstacles getting in my way!"*

London went into the kitchen getting one of Kenya's peach flavored wine coolers out of the refrigerator. She hated the way that they tasted, but holding the bottle in her hand made her feel more mature. Plus, most of the females in the nasty uncut videos all had glasses in their hands as they danced around.

"Where is he at?" She wondered watching the clock. Sitting down on the couch, crossing her legs, London held the remote in her right hand clicking channels while tapping the cooler bottle with the left.

◉

O.T. pulled into the driveway and turned off his car. He sat back in the custom leather bucket seats, leaning his neck on the headrest. O.T. had to collect his thoughts and closed his eyes briefly. Seeing his brother still suffering after all this time was causing him to have constant migraine headaches. As much as he tried being the strong person that all the people involved depended on, he was starting to crack from the heavy stressed filled pressure.

When he sat up, opening up his eyes, O.T. saw Kenya standing in the doorway waving to him. "Damn, I guess I should go ahead and go in." He mumbled as he unlocked the car door.

Getting closer up towards the door, he busted out laughing. "Oh shit, tell me I'm seeing thangs!" O.T. stopped in his tracks folding his arms and started shaking his head. The jersey he was wearing showed off every muscle, his jeans sagged perfectly and his Tims had the tongue stuck out with the laces loose. "What's so funny?" London asked with her hands firmly on her hips. She had done her best to imitate Kenya and now O.T. was standing there laughing in her face. "What's wrong? You don't like it?" London stood still as she waited for him to speak.

"Ain't shit funny Ma. Ain't shit funny at all." He rubbed his chin licking his lips. "I just thought that you was Kenya and shit. My mistake, don't trip!"

"I'm not tripping, but I don't want you making fun of me." London whined.

"Dig dis here." He cut her off. "Where is Kenya at anyway? Is she up there with Storm?"

London stopped pouting and giggled. "She's not home. She went somewhere with Paris. Don't you and your girl communicate?"

"Don't worry about my girl okay? That ain't none of ya business." O.T. got closer kissing her on the lips. "Well what is my business?"

"This right here should be you main concern right about now!" O.T. put her hand on his dick and backed her into the living room. It was just like Christmas and his birthday all wrapped into one. He had his hands roaming her entire body. London's skirt was pushed up exposing the fact that she didn't have any panties on. Her naked ass looked just as he had imagined, perfect, plump and round.

After feeling on, across and in every part of her body, O.T. was ready to get to the real deal. When he pulled his dick out of his jeans, London was amazed. His shit was long and thick. The head was lighter than the rest of it and was dripping. "Come get this Ma. He wants to meet you" He motioned to her with one hand slowly stroking his manhood.

"Do you have any protection?" London wisely asked.

"Naw, I'm good. I ain't got no diseases!"

"I didn't say that you did, but I would feel a lot better if we used something." London spoke up as she broke free from his arms and ran upstairs to try to find a rubber in some of Kenya's belongings.

Five long minutes passed and London hadn't returned yet with the condom. An anxious O.T. sprinted up the staircase and bumped into London, who was coming out of Storm and Kenya's room. He held her tightly and began kissing her once again.

She was breathing hard from searching the dresser drawers and was like a rag doll when he took his mouth off of hers. O.T.'s pants were still unzipped making it easy for him to pull his semi-hard dick back out. He propped his body inside the doorway for support and pushed London down on her knees. Using both of his hands he took her head in between them and guided her mouth onto to the head of his dripping stick. "Give him a wet kiss." He urged. "I haven't ever..." Her earring fell off from the force. "Ever what?" He halted her words by rubbing his dick across her lips making her taste his pre cum.

The gloss that she had applied earlier was now on the head of his shaft. London tried to keep protesting but was only met by O.T. placing his hand firmly behind her neck and the raw feeling of hard meat practically pounding her tonsils crooked.

London was starting to make gagging sounds that only fired O.T. up more. The more that London fought to breathe the harder he pushed in and out.

In all the erotic chaos that was taking place, the two of them failed to realize that for a few brief seconds, Storm had regained conscious and reached out his hand towards them.

O.T. was at the point of no return and yelled out Paris' name not London's as he shot the mother load down throat making sure that she swallowed it all. When he released her out his grip, London fell onto the plush new smelling carpet grasping for air. Before she could regain her composure, O.T.'s phone chirped. It was Paris saying that it was an emergency and to meet her at their house ASAP.

"I gotta go! My Baby needs me!" He stepped over London's body with his Tims still on, to get a wet rag. O.T. then zipped up his pants on the way down the stairs leaving a confused and emotionally drained wounded London on the floor alone whimpering.

"Please don't go." She quietly begged. "Please." O.T. hadn't paid a second thought to anything that was being said. From the moment he got the call from Paris saying 911, nothing else mattered. "I'll be back to see Storm! And thanks for that head shot!"

London heard him slam the front door shut and the sound of the music from his car stereo fade out of ear range. After a short while she went to the bathroom.

◎

London washed her face and brushed her teeth twice trying to get the smell of O.T.'s thick hot sperm out her mouth. Every time she swallowed it seemed like there was a strange after taste lingering.

She couldn't believe that O.T. had the nerve to shout out another woman's name while they were doing something, well at least while she was. London was totally pissed off, but not at him for that out cold callous display but at Paris for interrupting them with her false problems.

London knew that Kenya would soon be on her way home so she rushed to Storm's bedside to give him his medication. She didn't want to hear Kenya's long dragged out arguing about anything tonight. She wasn't in the mood, her throat was still hurting.

The syringe was only one third of the way filled as London walked over to the I.V. bag that was hanging. She laid the needle down on the night stand for a quick second, to get one of the moist wipes out the drawer and wet Storm's dry lips. Time was ticking and she still had to change to her own clothes. As she reached over and started to touch Storm's face with the wipe he raised his arm up all of a sudden and grabbed her wrist.

"Kenya, how could you?" He managed to say.

"Stop! You're hurting me!" A stunned London tried pulling back. "Let me go!"

"Why Kenya? Why did you lie to me?" Storm was now applying pressure to London's tiny wrist.

"I'm not Kenya, I'm London!" She argued.

"First you were Tastey, then Kenya and now you're London!" Storm had tears in his eyes. "I thought that you loved me? You said you did!"

"I'm not Kenya I keep telling you! Now let me loose." London tried prying his fingers off her.

"You're not Kenya, but you're wearing the outfit that I picked out for her in Vegas. You smell just like cucumber melon, her favorite scent and if you haven't looked in the mirror lately, you look just like Kenya!" Storm was heated as he confronted who he truly believed was Kenya. "Stop denying it. Your lies won't work any more. Just tell me why?"

"Please Storm, you're hurting me!" London pleaded.

"You hurt me to!" Storm argued. "And I see the shit ain't stopped. I woke up and called out to you and what the fuck do I see, but my suppose to be fiancee and the love of my life on her knees deep throating my baby brother." Storm snatched London by her neck. He was furious and wouldn't listen to a word that was coming out of London's mouth. "I outta snap this motherfucker in two. You ain't shit!"

London got the strength some how and yanked away stumbling to the floor. "You're crazy!" She screamed running out the room. "You're crazy!"

Storm tried his best to get out the bed and chase after her, but couldn't. His busted leg wouldn't let him. "Kenya! Kenya! Kenya!" He kept calling out in vain. "Come back here! Kenya come back!"

The echoing sound of his voice and the thought of what he had witness between her and O.T. was too much for London to stand. She ran out onto the front porch to escape his verbal wrath.

Ten minutes later Paris pulled up letting Kenya out the car and drove off in a rush. Kenya strolled up the walkway and found London perched on the stairs. "What are you doing sitting out here?" Kenya's facial expression changed when she got a good look at her twin sister. "And why the hell do you have on my fucking clothes? Storm bought me that damn outfit! Go take it the fuck off!"

As Kenya waited for her answer, London grew angry at the fact that everything always had to be about Kenya. She twisted her upper lip and grinned. "You always think that you and your girl, Paris are so high and mighty don't you?"

"What that got to do with why you wearing my stuff?" Kenya fumed. "Tell me that!"

"Whatever!" London ignored her sister.

"Well, I'm waiting." Kenya tapped her foot. "Why do you have my shit on your back and my new shoes on your feet? Are you gonna answer me or what?"

London stood up rubbing her sore wrist that was starting to bruise and let her twin have it. "I'll tell you what Kenya. I've got a bright ideal for you. Why don't you go your uppity, stuck up, trying to forget where you came from ass inside the house and try answering some questions your damn self?"

"What are you talking about?" Kenya was puzzled by her sisters' statement. "What do you mean?"

"What I mean is that you should stop worrying so much about your damn precious little clothes that I borrowed and go in there." London pointed towards the door. "Your foolish ass boyfriend, Storm is wide awake and seems to be somewhat in his right mind. And if I'm not mistaken, something tells me he wants to see you."

"Oh my God! Move outta my way!" Kenya ran passed London and up to her and Storm's bedroom. She could hear him screaming out her name louder with each step she took.

It was now time for Kenya to face him, explain her ridiculous un-necessary lies and try her best to make shit right again.

YOU DIRTY BITCH

Kenya neared the door of the bedroom almost coming to a complete stop. She leaned against the wall taking several deep breaths. Her pulse was racing and a sudden feeling of jitters caused her to tear up. Kenya's ears were filled with the echoing of Storm's enraged yells.

"Kenya! Kenya!" He ranted. "Where the fuck are you at? Don't let me get out of this motherfucking bed! I'm not playing with your ass!"

She was frozen with denial. Kenya had never once, since meeting Storm, heard him even raise his voice at her. Now he was lying a few feet away injured and messed up in the bed, sounding like he was ready to break his foot off into her ass.

"Damn! I can't put this shit off any longer. It ain't gonna do nothing but make matters worse." After one more deep breath Kenya turned the corner going in.

"Oh, I see your stanking ass finally decide to come back huh?" Storm's hands were clenched onto the blanket that was on the bed. "I know you heard me calling you!"

Kenya was quiet, not believing the words that were flying out of Storm's mouth. She couldn't move out the doorway as he continued to go off.

"If my leg wasn't fucked up it would be me and you hoe! And mostly me! Believe that!" Storm struggled to get up without success, finally resting his weak body back on the mattress. "Bring your no good dick sucking ass over here!" He demanded firmly.

Kenya remained still as tears of pain flowed down her face. She had no response to him and his insults. She felt guilty enough. Kenya had no defense because if she'd only been honest from the jump maybe some if not all the crap that her man had to suffer and endure could've been avoided totally.

"I said come here bitch! I swear to God I ain't gonna ask you no more Kenya!"

"Listen Storm." She got the courage to say. "I can explain everything if you just give me a chance."

"We been together for months on top of months. You had all the time in the world to confess your double rotten ass life and now you wanna be calm and talk."

"But…" Kenya tried to speak.

"But what bitch? What the fuck can you say?"

"Please Storm!"

"Please Storm what?" He argued as he pounded his closed fist into the mattress. "Please don't be mad that I'm a back stabbing little whore? Is that what you wanna say after all this time?"

Once again Kenya grew silent. She still hadn't got within reach of Storm's bed side in fear of what he might actually do. Staring down at the carpet as she cried she saw one of her earrings on the floor. It was the mate to the one that London was wearing. She made a mental note to check her sister later on, knowing damn well that this wasn't the time.

"I guess you playing the dumb dumb role now. Well I'll tell you what Kenya, consider all the fake games as over." Storm swallowed slowly trying to regain his composure. "You ain't gotta say shit. After all the writing is already on the wall. Just know that because of you and your scheming, I hate dope dealers ass, I damn near got killed."

"Are you going to give me at least a chance to try to make you see my side in all of this?" Kenya tried reasoning. "Please Storm. I'm begging you."

"What you gonna tell me huh?" He laughed as Kenya gathered up the nerve to get closer to the man that she loved with all of her heart. "You gonna tell me that you ain't know nothing about that P.A.I.D. bull shit right? You gonna tell me that you ain't trying to under mind my entire operation and shut shit down right? Is that what you bout to say hoe?"

Storm reached out and yanked Kenya onto the bed with him. She didn't try to resist, feeling like if he kicked her ass and got it out his system, maybe then he'd give her a chance to explain. Kenya was willing to make any sacrifice that it took to get things back to normal, even if it meant getting beat the fuck down in her own bed without putting up a fight.

Storm tossed her around the king size bed with rage as he kept the questions and harsh accusations coming. "What's wrong Kenya? I don't hear you telling me anymore of those lies about you loving me so much!" He yelled as spit flew in her face.

Kenya didn't once scream or try to get away from the assault.

"I guess you played me from the jump huh?" Storm ripped Kenya's shirt off of her back exposing her red laced bra. The sight of her plump breast usually excited him, but this time was much different. After seeing O.T.'s hands rubbing and feeling on them earlier as she sucked his dick, Storm wanted to throw up. He smacked Kenya across her jaw with all his force. She flew out the bed and hit the floor dazed and dizzy.

"I guess you ain't London Roberts either with your good snitching rat ass?" Storm was pissed and out of control, as he threw the lamp off the night stand at Kenya's head. "And I guess you wasn't just down on the floor swallowing my little brothers dick damn near whole in front of my face!"

The bedroom door flung open, causing both Kenya and Storm to turn and wait for the shit to hit the fan. The next round was sure to be worse than the first.

"Is that you O.T.?" Storm asked as he wiped the sweat off his forehead. "Is it?"

Kenya planned on breaking the news about her twin sister, but fuck it. She was now here to do it herself.

"No it's not your henpecked little brother! It's me, London Roberts. The same London Roberts who was sucking his dick! Is that okay with you?" London stood with her hands on her hips. "And if you touch my sister like that again I'm going to kill you with my bare hands!"

Storm's eyes seemed to be jumping out of their sockets. He rubbed them both thinking that he must be hallucinating from the medication that they were keeping him doped up on. "I don't understand. What the fuck is going on?" He placed his palm on his forehead to check for a fever. "Kenya, who is she? I mean which one of you is Kenya? I'm confused. What's going on? What are yall trying to do to me?" Storm started to hyperventilate from the shock and stress. His body was still weak from his injuries and couldn't take the overly exhausting turmoil that was taking place. He passed out cold.

◉

It was a couple of hours later when Storm finally regained conscious. O.T. was sitting on the edge of the bed and laughing as his brother woke up. "Open up your eyes faggot ass sleeping beauty. I ain't got all day to be waiting around to kick your butt in the new Madden!"

Storm was still slightly weak, but managed to sit up and get off into O.T.'s ass. "Later for all that. Man, where the fuck is Kenya at? I had one of the most craziest dreams in the world or should I say fucking nightmares. It was two of them bitches!"

"Hold up dude, that wasn't no dream. It is." O.T. got his brother a cold glass of water to drink while he explained. "Your woman got an identical twin sister. Her name is London and trust me you can't hardly tell them the fuck apart! She been living back in Detroit all this time." O.T. shrugged his shoulders and rubbed his head. "Why didn't she tell you about her? Kenya is straight out of order!"

"Fuck all that bull! Where is she at?" Storm asked loudly. "I don't believe all that twin stuff!"

"Who London?"

"Hell naw Kenya!" Storm frowned. "Matter of fact, yeah go get both of them." He still didn't think that it could be possible that Kenya had a sister, let alone a twin sister. "Show me both of them side by side!"

O.T. left out the room and walked downstairs to inform the girls that Storm was awake.

"Hey Kenya, he's up, but ole boy don't think that it's two of yall. He thinks that he was just bugging out on all that medication that Big Doc B got him on. He wanna see you and London, together."

"Well to fucking bad! I don't want to see that no good female beating brother of yours!" London rolled her eyes as she kept a cold wet rag pressed onto Kenya's swollen face. "After what he did to my sister I should call the damn police and press charges on him!" She leaped to her feet with anger.

"Bitch! I wish you would call 5-0 on Storm!"

O.T. was now standing toe to toe with London who wasn't in the mood for backing down. She still had a beef with him from earlier. Also sitting in the living room with a permanent grim expression was Paris.

O.T. and Paris had been feuding ever since she stepped foot back inside their house. O.T. had the nerve to try to lie about being at the mall with Chocolate Bunny. Even after Paris described stitch by stitch everything that the slut was wearing he still denied it. Paris knew that her girl Jordan saw his ass, no doubt about it, but she wasn't gonna put her on front street. Paris had just enough time to smack the shit out of O.T. and brace up to battle with his lunatic butt, when the call came in that Storm was awake and asking for him. The two promised to settle things up later that night as they rushed over.

Paris got up in O.T.'s face daring him to put his hands on London, Kenya or her. O.T. decided to try to reason with the hostile females, mainly Kenya.

"Listen, I don't know if all three of yall is bleeding or what, but you gotta expect for Storm to be trippin' right about now!" O.T. leaned over and looked Kenya in her eyes. "Don't none of us know what the fuck he had to go through. That nigga been shot, leg fucked the hell up, ear sliced and almost starved to death and you hoes wanna bug out!"

Kenya was starting to feel remorse for having an attitude that Storm had kicked her ass without giving her a chance to talk. "I guess you're right O.T." She removed the rag from her black and blue bruised jaw and got up off the couch. "Please London, can you just go up there with me to see him for a minute?"

London folded her arms and turned her focus on the green grass and flowers that were right outside the huge picture window. She ignored her sisters' request, acting as if the devil himself had ask for help burning Bibles on Easter Sunday.

"Get ya punk ass up them damn stairs before I drag you up there!" O.T. pushed London.

"Paris, I strongly suggest you get your coward so called man before I say something that everyone will regret." London caught her self from falling into the sofa table. "Now that I think about it…"

Kenya remembered all the accusations that Storm made, including going down on O.T. and the fact that London owned up to it and even seemed proud. Kenya knew her twin's personality had turned foul.

She was in pain and sore as a motherfucker, but knew that if London let that lil cat out the bag, everybody in the house would be thumping. "Please London, I'm begging you. I'll do anything you want me to do. Just come on!" Kenya pulled her sister by the arm and led her up the staircase. London turned back giving O.T. the evil eye as she watched Paris start to argue with him.

The twins were almost at the bedroom door, when Kenya stopped and whispered in London's ear. "I know you and O.T. was fucking around this afternoon and that shit was rotten as hell and me and you can kick it about that tonight, but you got to promise me that no matter what, you won't go off on Storm. He was confused and he's still in so much pain, physically and mentally." Kenya held both of London's hands. "Please London be calm. For me!"

"All right for you Kenya and only you, I'll be on my best behavior, because as far as Storm and O.T. are concerned I'm pass done!"

The twins joined hands as they slowly walked into the bedroom making eye contact with Storm.

◉

PARIS

"Damn O.T., why you always gotta go for bad all the time? Especially when it comes to females! Shit already fucked up enough without you trying to fight Kenya's sister." Paris was sick and tired of him and his wild ways. "I bet you don't be all posted up in that nasty tramp Chocolate Bunny's face with that madness, do you?"

O.T. leaned back on the loveseat and sucked his teeth like a woman. "I already told ya ass I don't know what the fuck ya talking about, so stop jumping to conclusions and blaming me for shit I ain't do before I ready do fuck her black ass again!"

"You can do what the hell you want to do, but remember two can play that game." Paris took her purse off of the coffee table and nonchalantly made her way to the front door. "So think about that the next time your smart ass goes Missing In Action!" Paris started up her car and sped away leaving O.T. looking dumb as a fuck.

"Kick rocks bitch!" He mumbled walking upstairs.

IT'S TRUE

"Hi Storm." Kenya spoke in a low soft tone. "O.T. told me that you wanted to see me or should I say us." She pointed to London.

Storm sat all the way up in the bed and wiped his eyes. "Come here Kenya. Come closer so I can see."

The twins held each other's arms as they carefully approached Storm who was shaking his head. He squinted as the girls came closer to the light. "Shit! What kinda crap is this?"

"Storm, I'm so sorry that I didn't tell you about London." Kenya begged getting on her knees at the edge on the bed. "I just didn't think that you'd understand."

"Why not? Have I ever given you a reason to fear me Kenya? Have I ever tried to control you?"

"No." She shamelessly dropped her head to avoid eye contact with him, letting her hair drape over her distraught battered face. "Never once Storm."

"Then why?" He asked keeping his sight glued to London as he questioned Kenya. "What was the big fucking deal? Can you tell me that?"

The sound of him raising his voice caused London to speak up and intervene on her sisters' behalf. "It seems as if to me that you have some kind of anger management issues. That trait must run in your family." London sarcastically added. "My sister probably didn't tell you about me because she figured that you would disapprove of anyone that wasn't agreeable with your criminal behavior."

"Oh yeah, is that right?" He fired back. "It appears that way to me, especially by the looks of Kenya's face, you freaking animal!"

Storm had momentary forgotten about the ass kicking that he'd put on his girl. He reached over touching Kenya on her chin. "Look up at me."

She obliged hesitantly moving the hair out her face exposing the damage that would take days to heal. "Damn Kenya! I'm sorry! I didn't mean to do all of that. You just caught me off guard." He then pulled her off the floor and onto the bed with him.

"Kenya! Don't fall for that I'm sorry routine! If he hit you like that once he'll do it again!" London tried her best to discourage her twin from forgiving him.

"Why don't you try shutting the fuck up? It's your fault all this shit went down!" Storm hissed.

"My fault? Are you sick in the head? I'm not the one out here running the streets' poisoning the damn community!" London yelled loud enough to wake the dead. "That would be you and your no good brother that's guilty of that crime!"

Storm tilted his head towards the side and had a flashback. "You mean the same brother that I saw you getting your knees dirty for earlier?"

London was slightly ashamed but continued her words coming. "Yeah that's him. The same one that can get out the bed and take a piss on his own! Not like you!" She teased with malice. "Bed wetter!"

"Kenya, I want this trouble making whore out my motherfucking house!" Storm tried to get up.

"Why don't you put me out?" London challenged.

"Bitch, get the fuck out! I'm not playing around with your stanking wanna be the police ass!"

Kenya stood up and broke up the below the belt insults that were taking place between London and Storm. "Listen London, why don't you go back downstairs and let me speak to Storm privately? And Storm why don't you try to calm down before you pass out again?"

"Okay Kenya. I'll be in the living room."

"Try being out on the curb!" Storm hissed as London made her exit.

Almost at the end of the hallway she met O.T. who was busy talking to him self.

"Excuse me!" She bumped his arm.

"Why the hell is you bugging? I thought me and you was tight! What's the problem?"

London couldn't believe that O.T. was so dense in the brain that he was truly convinced that his cold heartless actions from earlier in the afternoon were acceptable. She went straight ghetto on him. "Okay Negro! I'll tell you what the problem is!" She pointed her index finger in his face. "If you think that you're gonna just mess around and toy with my feelings and emotions, you've got another thing coming buster!"

"Whoa! Slow the fuck down!" He pushed her hand away. "I had to go. You heard Paris chirp me!"

"And?" London waited.

"And what? My girl needed me and I jetted. What else did you expect me to do?"

"Maybe show some type of love towards me!"

"Come on now London. Don't act like me and you is in some type of real relationship." O.T. stepped back throwing his hands in the air. "You knew that Paris was Wifey from the rip! She's number one!"

London was hurt once again as reality spit in her face. "Whatever! Ain't nobody thinking about you!" She marched pass O.T. and stomped down the stairs. "Bitches!" He laughed out loud as he went to check on Storm and Kenya.

When O.T. peeped in he saw that she was next to Storm holding his hand. They seemed to be in deep discussion so he didn't disturb them. O.T. went into the den and laid back on the couch as he looked over in the corner where the aquarium once sat that served as a final resting spot for Deacon's head.

"Damn I'm gonna hate to tell Storm about Deacon!"

◉

It was now dark outside. It had started to thunder and pour buckets of rain making the night seem to drag by. Storm and Kenya had been talking for hours trying to get their lives back on track. Everything that she was holding in about her former life, he was now aware of. From the first morning she skipped school, Ty turning her out on the dance game and even the fact that she pocketed the money that him and Deacon paid to Zack after her Uncle and his crew shot up Heads Up. Kenya's life was an open book.

Storm had no other choice but to confess about shit that he was holding back on also. Kenya sat silent as he talked about his mother's crack habit, which he never did. She was stunned to learn that Storm had did time in a juvenile facility for killing his step-father and worse that anything else he revealed that he, O.T. and Deacon had all slept with Chocolate Bunny at one time or another back in the day. Kenya knew that O.T. had fucked the bitch, but not Deacon and certainly not Storm. Her hands were tied.

What could she say, after all the terrible secrets and lies she was tangled up into. Kenya had to remain calm and be understanding even though she couldn't wait until she bumped heads with Chocolate Bunny again. All the 'try to chill' information that she always begged Paris to do, was out the window.

By the time that they were finished, Storm agreed to let London stay temporary until all the bullshit was done and over. Kenya knew that it was gonna be a lot of fussing and confusion, but she loved both of them and wanted them both in her life.

Storm wanted to talk to O.T. about Deacon because Kenya kept avoiding any and all questions that involved Deacon's name. She went in the hallway and called out for O.T. When he finally showed up, Kenya informed him that Storm wanted to see him and was asking about whether or not there had been any information concerning Deacon.

O.T. entered the room and delivered the fucked up devastating news of Deacon's callous torture and murder. When it was all said and done, Storm could only say one thing. "I need a motherfucking drink!"

MAD CRAZY

The months flew by and things only grew wilder and crazier by the moment. Storm was still in constant pain and hadn't stepped foot outside of the crib. He would have Kenya bring him home Tylenol 4's on the regular and kept a bottle of Remy up to his lips. Even though Kenya would often beg and plead with Storm not to drink so much, especially while he was popping those pills, it was no use. He was addicted and had started blacking out daily. His leg was still weak, so that meant that he was depended on the aid of crutches, which fucked with his mental mind.

The fact that Storm was having trouble getting his dick hard was a major factor in his recovery. Most times he'd have to damn near beat his meat to death or choke and twist it to just make the motherfucker pee. So him and Kenya fucking like they used to was out of the picture all together, driving him to drink harder. Of course London used that information to her advantage to taunt and tease Storm when he and she argued. What kinda come back or response could any man have to that type of dis?

Kenya would clean up behind Storm all day and manage Alley Cats at night. She was exhausted and drained each and every time her head would touch the pillow. She was nurse, maid, cook and lastly referee between the still constantly battling London and Storm. Her once clear skin was now filled with pimples and dark bags were under her eyes.

O.T. and Paris were still beefing. The shit seemed to never stop with them. O.T. was out running the streets harder than before. With Storm putting his own ass on house arrest that left O.T. to try to keep thangs pumping. That meant that every drop off, every meeting and every risk that went along with slinging dope was on his shoulders. In between trying to be the self-proclaimed Mayor of the Hood, he still would squeeze in time to swing by and check on Storm. Those visits often would cause mad chaos to jump off at the condo when O.T. would see London.

Kenya knowing what she knew was still on a strong mission to keep O.T. and London apart. She talked to a depressed and tear filled Paris every night as she drove to the club. After the confrontation that she'd had at the hair salon with Chocolate Bunny, Kenya felt it best for the good of the club to let Paris go. After all it was only a temporary gig, so there were no hard feelings between the friends.

With O.T. gone so much Paris would sit on the couch for hours at a time watching old reruns of Good Times and stuffing her self full of candy, cookies and chips waiting for him to come back home.

London was having the time of her life as she sharpen her vocabulary skills Monday thru Sunday, dusk to dawn on an educationally disadvantaged Storm. They would find a reason to argue about, rather the sun was shinning at midnight or how many licks it really took to get to the middle of a tootsie pop. All it took for the shit to be on was for the two to lay eyes on one another. For London, getting and remaining on Storm's bad side was second nature. She seemed to despise him.

Kenya felt that it was time for her sister to go back to Detroit or rather back to school since the sale of the house was now final, but would never suggest it. Besides, they were keeping Storms return kinda secret from the niggas in the streets and with her and O.T. out and about, trying to hold shit down, there was no one else that they trusted to keep somewhat of a watchful eye over Storm, especially with his blacking out.

◙

FATE

It started off just like any other Friday night. Kenya was busy standing in the mirror brushing her hair and getting prepared to head out to Alley Cats. She had on a pair of tight fitting blue jeans and a blue and pink low cut t-shirt with the words 'Hot Shit' across the chest. Even with make up on you could still see that she was worn out. Storm was laying, half a sleep, in the bed with the television remote in his hand. An empty bottle of Remy Martin was on the floor next to two forties of Old English that were also bone dry.

Storm was up to his usual behavior, getting drunk and passing out. He hadn't shaved in days and him taking a shower was almost an impossible feat. The entire room and house for that matter smelled like a roadhouse. Kenya prayed that with time Storm would snap out of the destructive path that he was on and get his life back together.

"Okay Sweetheart, I'm about to go down to the club." She nudged him on his arm. "Do you need me to get you something before I leave?"

"Yeah, just you Kenya! I want some pussy!" He grabbed out for her almost falling out the bed.

Kenya helped him up and played his request off knowing that it had been months since he'd been home and his dick still couldn't get hard. She had no intentions on being late to the club because of one of Storm's pity parties that he was about to throw. "I'll be home later. Why don't you go soak in the tub and chill out?"

"Why don't you bring me up another bottle of liquor and shut up your damn nagging?" He slurred.

"Not a problem!" Kenya made her way into the den.

"Hey London!" Kenya smiled as she saw her twin sitting at the desk typing on the computer. "I'm about to leave and go to work. I know that this is asking a lot, but can you run to the store and get him something to drink?" Kenya pointed towards her bedroom. "I'm late enough already."

"Don't you think that he's already had enough to drink for you, me and the whole world?" London threw her hand up in her sisters' face. "Your Prince Charming has turned into the Village Idiot!"

"Please London! For me!" Kenya pleaded.

"Yeah okay, let me get off the Internet with Fatima." Kenya walked pass the open bedroom door without turning her head to say goodbye to Storm.

◎

London went into the kitchen to put away a few of the items that she bought from the corner store when she picked up a Fifth for Storm. As she was bending down in the refrigerator to put the sodas on the door she felt hands snatch her body roughly knocking her to the marble floor. Her head struck the corner of the oak cabinet making her woozy and confused.

When she gained her senses back, she started to fight and struggle with a drunken enraged hallucinating Storm who was on top of her licking her face. The more she wiggled and moved to get free, the greater pleasure he seemed to achieve.

"Don't fight me Kenya!" He screamed in London's face with his nauseating foul smelling breath. "I told you Daddy wanted some. Now give it to me!"

"I'm not Kenya fool! Get off of me!"

"I love you! Why you acting like this after all I done did for you? Now give me some pussy!"

Storm protested London's words and tried wrapping one of his huge hands across her mouth to silence having to hear anymore complaining. London's eyes grew wide and bucked as her sisters' fiancee held her down with the weight of his body as he made use of his free hand to pull down his track pants so that his dick was dangling wildly between his and London's legs. She tried to knee him in the nuts but was stopped by the force of him applying his total strength on her.

"Are you crazy! Stop! Stop! Don't do this! Stop!"

Storm was in some sort of a trance. It was like he was sleep walking and totally unaware of his surroundings. His eyes rolled to the back of his head as he ripped London's shorts down and somehow shoved his hard dick up in her. It was the first true 100%, staying hard, can fuck the shit out of you all night erection that he had since being home and here he was on the kitchen floor, drunk as a son of a bitch with Kenya's sisters legs stretched wide open.

He acted like a mad man as he went in and out of her overly moist pussy. All of London's out cries of her not being Kenya had come to a halt. She stopped resisting Storm and even seemed to start to enjoy what she was feeling. She closed her eyes and imagined that he was O.T. making love to her.

After fifteen minutes of Storm doing his thang he let out a yell as his body jerked and collapsed onto London's. He passed out cold, not moving an inch.

Reality quickly set back in for her when the rotten smelling musk of Storm's skin filled her nostrils. The ecstasy that she was just felling had ended and now London wanted her sworn enemy the hell off of her.

She managed to push his heavy body off onto the cold floor and got up on her feet. The sight of Storm sprawled out, smelling like who done it and why, caused London to rush over to the sink and throw up all over the dishes.

"Damn! That felt good, but why did it have to be him? Stuff wasn't supposed to work out like this."

London mumbled to herself as she stepped over his crutches that were blocking the door and walked out the kitchen to take a hot shower, leaving a snoring Storm to sleep his punk ass on the floor.

"But I sure now see why Kenya is putting up with all the crap that Storm is taking her through."

A NEW DAY

The days that followed that night somehow brought about a drastic change in Storm's personality. He'd been woke up at four in the morning, by Kenya returning home from work. He felt like warm melted shit on a stick. Storm had no ideal how he'd gotten downstairs let alone on the floor.

As he passed the huge oval shaped mirror in the hallway. Storm caught a quick glance of him self and froze with disappointment. He saw a complete stranger staring back at him. It was then and there that he promised Kenya that he was gonna get his shit back right.

When he hugged Kenya his dick rose up standing at attention. The two of them made their way up the stairs and into their bedroom. Kenya turned the shower on hot as she helped Storm step inside. He spent hours scrubbing months of filth off his ass.

The combination of the soap and the hot water caused a scratch on the back of his neck to sting. When he closed his eyes he kept seeing flashbacks of fucking Kenya on the kitchen floor. He knew that it must've been a dream so he dismissed it out of his mind.

No sooner than he was finished drying off, he pounced on top of Kenya making love to her for the first time in months. She was in seventh heaven as he freaked her from head to toe. Kenya, unlike Storm who just had some pussy earlier, hadn't had sex in what seemed like twelve months of Sundays and was really feeling that shit.

They fucked till almost daybreak while London listened to their loud moans from the other room.

◉

For weeks and weeks Storm stuck to his word and stopped drinking. The only fluid that was now constantly up to his lips were ice cold water and the juices that flowed out of Kenya's forever wet pussy. O.T. had helped him hook the basement up with weights and other gym equipment that he needed.

He spent every free moment on getting his body tight. As the days passed he was gaining back the pounds that he'd loss and looking like the old Storm that Kenya first fell in love with.

Even, to Kenya's surprise, London was being much more tolerant and civil to Storm. The two of them weren't arguing as much and London was helping Kenya with the housework more often.

Poor Kenya had no ideal that the reason London was lending a helpful hand was so that she could smell Storm's shirts and dirty underwear. The high point of London's day would come when she'd carry the laundry basket in the basement to wash and get a show of Storm's perfect body pumping iron.

◉

"Girl, thanks for looking out for me with some of this cleaning." Kenya hugged her twin happy that things were settling down. "You know Gran blessed you with all the secrets in keeping a neat house."
"Oh it's nothing." London winked her eye.
"Yes it is, I want you to know that you're really appreciated and that I love you London!"

"We sisters!" London gave Kenya a half-hearted smile. "You should know by now that I've got your back."

The two finished getting the condo together because they were having a special dinner later that evening. It would be Kenya, Storm, Paris, O.T. and London. Kenya trusted in the changes that were taking place in London when it came to O.T. It seemed just like a snap of the fingers, London was no longer attracted to O.T. It would be days when O.T. stopped by to hang out with Storm that London wouldn't even come out of her room. She stayed sleep most days.

Whatever jumped off to keep the two of them from fucking around again behind Paris' back, Kenya was overjoyed. She never did get around to having a long conversation with London about what really went down the day that Storm saw her and O.T. in the hallway, so Kenya let her imagination work for its self. Putting two and two together was easy.

But never the less things were back on track all around with the small exception of the Paris, O.T., Chocolate Bunny Saga, which was a hot topic.

◉

The table was set and everything was perfect for the evening. Kenya, with London's help cooked enough food to feed a small sized army. The huge celebration feast consisted of everything from hot country fried chicken, beef pot roast smothered in homemade brown gravy and catfish to fresh collard greens, candied yams and black eyed peas. The girls had out done themselves.

Paris and O.T. arrived to the condo on time. They planned on having an early supper because Kenya was due down at the club by eight that evening. She tried to get someone to fill in for her, but had no success.

O.T. disappeared into the basement where Storm was just finishing up his workout, leaving all three females alone in the kitchen area.

"Hey Paris." London spoke as she inspected her sister's best friend. Paris had packed on at least fifteen pounds or more since London had last seen her. "What have you been up to lately?"

"Not much." Paris shrugged her shoulders.

"Oh, it's just that I haven't saw you around here much." London quizzed still stunned by Paris' big physical change. "Is all well with you?"

Kenya saw the direction that her twin was headed and jumped in to rescue Paris from all the questions. "Do me a favor London." Kenya wiped her hands on the plaid colored dish towel. "Can you go and call the fellas while me and Paris start bringing the food to the table?"

"Yeah, I can do that." London happily left to go in the basement. If she was lucky maybe Storm still had his shirt off. The smells of the food were making her dizzy anyway as well as the heat from the oven.

When London was clearly out of ear range, Kenya apologized for her twin sister being so damn nosey. "Girl, she didn't mean to be all up in ya shit like that. She just was concerned that's all."

Paris grabbed one of the china trays with the chicken on it and headed towards the dinning room. "Don't worry. I don't mind. I guess I do look like a mess with all this extra weight that I'm hauling."

"Stop trippin'. You tight Paris."

Kenya followed behind her friend with a big bowl of greens in her hands.

"You don't have to lie. I know that this fat shit ain't cute." Paris lowered her head on the verge of tears.

"Stop being so down on yourself."

"I can't help it Kenya! Do you know that O.T. hasn't touched me in over two and a half weeks now?"

Kenya hugged her friend as she sobbed. "He barely even comes to the crib until daybreak. He claims that he's out hustlin', but I know that nigga is lying."

Before Kenya got a chance to hear the entire story, London returned with both guys trailing behind. "Damn that shit smells good!" Storm rubbed his flat stomach as took a seat at the head of the long marble table. "I'm bout to throw the fuck down!"

O.T. followed his brother's lead and sat at the other end. After all the food was laid out and the girls sat down, Storm blessed the gathering before the first fork was placed to any ones lips. Two or three seconds after that the shit was on! The guys acted like they'd never had soul food before as the devoured everything that they piled on their plates.

The only dinner conversation that was taking place consisted of girl talk and the sounds of grunting.

It was close to seven and the group was just about done with eating. Kenya was bringing an apple pie to the table for dessert when O.T.'s cell phone started to ring causing Paris to flip out.

"Damn! Can we have one day in peace when that hoe ain't blowing up your fucking phone?"

"Don't start with me Paris. I ain't in the mood for that dumb shit now!" O.T. walked away from the table. "I've got something to handle."

"Yeah right!" Paris reached back trying to hit him as he passed. "You ain't shit but a cheating liar."

Kenya leaned over and wrapped her arms around Storm who was still seated at the table. "Can you say something please?"

"I love you like a motherfucker Kenya, but I don't get in the middle of no couples bullshit." Storm cut him self a piece of pie as he remained silent watching his baby brother and Paris go at it.

London was especially enjoying the long evening observing both 'couples' at each other's throats.

At first she felt like a third wheel and out of place, now she was happy not to be either of the girls.

O.T. took Paris' car keys off the couch and trotted out to her car leaving her stranded without a ride to get home. "Damn, I hate him! I swear I do!" "Don't worry girl. I'll drop you off on my way to Alley Cats." Kenya patted her friend on the back as she snarled at Storm who was still stuffing his face with pie. "Just let me grab my purse." Paris and Kenya left London and Storm alone.

On the ride to drop her off at home, Kenya was having a hard time trying to console an almost hysterical Paris. The loud piercing cries were coming close to cause Kenya to swerve off the highway. She already needed a few aspirin for the headache she was suffering after her disagreement with Storm. "Why don't you go inside and try to rest? It's been a long day!" Kenya tried her best to convince Paris to calm the hell down, go lay down and relax.

"You right girl. I'm just gonna go in there and chill till his ass comes home, then trust, it's back on!" Kenya blew the horn once as she drove off.

◉

LONDON

"Dang, I guess this dinner party is over huh?" Storm was polishing off his last piece of pie that was on his plate not paying attention to a word out of London's mouth.

"Are you listening to me?" London threw a napkin at Storm. "Can you speak or what?"

"Slow ya roll London. Can a nigga eat his dessert in peace or what?" Storm pushed his chair back from the table and patted his bloated full stomach. "Well, I might as well go in the basement and do a little cardio to work this shit off."

"Excuse me. Despite what all of you guys around here think, I'm not the damn maid!" London grew infuriated that she was left the task of cleaning up.

"Where the hell is you going with this bullshit? I know ya ass know for a fact that I ain't about to bust no suds." Storm stretched out his arms and yawned.

"Forget it! Just go workout! With your lazy self!"

"Your ass is the one that needs to hit the gym. You getting a little thick around the waist London!"

"Go somewhere lazy Negro while I clean up!"

"Come on now London, is this the body of a lazy motherfucker?" He lifted his shirt exposing his abs. London controlled her self from leaping across the table and attacking Storm the same way he'd attacked her months earlier. "Whatever!" She looked the other way as quickly as possible and started removing the dishes taking them in the kitchen. Once again she started to feel dizzy.

Storm felt sorry for her and grabbed a few of the dirty plates and followed behind her. When he turned the corner he saw London bending over in the refrigerator putting stuff away and had a brief flashback. "Damn! Why do I keep seeing that shit?"

"Did you say something?" London stood up turning around to face him.

"Naw, I was just talking to myself." Storm shook off his strange thoughts as he rubbed the deep scar that was still on his neck.

"Does it still hurt?" London smirked starting the hot dish water in the sink. Her heart was beating double time as she experienced flashbacks of her own.

After all, they were back in the scene of the crime, so to speak.

"What you know about my damn neck?" Storm was puzzled that she'd even noticed him touch it.

"You can cut all the games out Storm. It has been months and you see I haven't said a word to anyone, except my friend Fatima."

Storm was confused and his facial expression showed. "Stop playing around and tell me what the fuck you trying to say?"

"Are you serious? You don't remember?" London glanced down at the floor and raised her eyebrows.

"Remember what?" He asked again.

"I've got to finish washing dishes." London laughed still not believing that Storm had truly forgotten their sexual encounter. "We'll talk later."

Storm left out the kitchen and headed towards the basement to try to figure out what his woman's twin sister wanted him to remember.

"Whatever the hell it is, it can't be nothing good!"

After months of being sober he snatched a bottle of Remy off the bar cart to keep him company.

I'M IN SHOCK

"Shit, it's crowed already." Kenya pulled around to the other side of the parking lot to make sure that security was patrolling the entire perimeter. She cut her lights off so she wouldn't draw attention to her self as she crept up. What she saw next made her head start to pound worse. It was O.T. sitting back in Paris' car talking to Chocolate Bunny who was leaning in the window practically in the drivers' seat.

 After five minutes of her watching their every movement like a hawk, Kenya wanted to beat the shit out of Chocolate Bunny her damn self. Matter of fact she wanted to stump O.T. in his fucking ball sack for playing her girl and fucking London. *"This nigga gonna mess around and get AIDS one day."* Kenya snarled under her breath, as she looked at Chocolate Bunny stuff some cash in her bra and wave to O.T. as he peeled out in Paris' car. *"Flat out, I gotta get rid of that black no good bitch."*

◎

"Hey Kenya, what's the game plan for tonight?" The head of security, Boz, was busy trying to get things straighten out before shit really got off the hook. "Same old same." She looked up towards the center stage, at Jordan shake her ass in front of a group of middle age customers, that were posted on perverts row. "Just make sure that all the girls circulate around the club and don't spend all night catering to one fool trying to slow pimp all his loot."

"You got it Boss. I'm on top of it!" He reassured Kenya. "Don't worry about shit."

Everything was flowing smoothly on the shift. Kenya sat at her favorite seat at the long bar and observed the crowd enjoyed themselves. Most of the dancers were either up in V.I.P. or humping on a guy's lap doing something strange for some change.

The D.J. was working the high priced light system and had the sounds spinning. "If you fellas nature stood tall and hard for that last honey that worked that brass pole, you'll love this next prime time delight. Alley Cats is home base to this dark meat.

She's the warmest, wettest, freakiest thang walking around these here parts." The D.J. dimmed the lights low. "Chocolate Bunny bring ya wide fluffy ass up on that center stage and do the damn thang!"

Kenya walked behind the bar and poured herself a glass of wine. She studied Chocolate Bunny dancing and wondered what it was that made men like her. In Kenya's opinion she wasn't sexy or cute. The only thing that Kenya saw in the hoe was that she had a big butt. A big butt that seemed to be spreading out a little bit more than normal.

"That tramp is gaining to much weight. I'm gonna give her trick ass a few weeks off to drop that shit or get fired." Kenya finally found a way after months of plotting, to get Chocolate Bunny out of Alley Cats. Each dancer had to maintain a certain look to be on the schedule. *"As soon as she goes back to the dressing room to switch up on her outfits, I'm gonna break the bad news to her trifling butt."*

Kenya raised her glass to her perfectly glossed lips and slowly sipped the rest of her wine. After two more songs Chocolate Bunny was done.

◉

CHOCOLATE BUNNY

"I'm happy for you." Jordan lied. "What are you going to name the baby? Is it a boy or a girl?"

"It's gonna be a boy. I'll probably name him after his big head daddy." Chocolate Bunny was in the dressing room bragging about being pregnant and the fact that her and her mystery man had just put a huge down payment on a new house.

She wasn't fooling everyone with all that top secret hush hush shit about the baby's daddy. All the girls in the club would see her all up in O.T.'s face day in and day out laughing and giggling. Jordan tried her best to pry the private information out of Chocolate Bunny or at least make her slip up and finally admit the shit, but wasn't successful.

"This week, is gonna be my last, grindin' in this here motherfucker. My man wants me to sit on my ass and raise his son." Chocolate Bunny stared down at the tiny bulge that was growing and smiled. "I'm ready to retire out this game anyway and get my life back together. Maybe I'll go back to school."

Kenya was at the doorway eavesdropping on the conversation that was taking place between Jordan and Chocolate Bunny. She felt like marching in the dressing room and knocking that bastard ass baby the fuck out the stomach of that man stealing black snake bitch, but what good would that really do?

Paris would be devastated whenever O.T. would be man enough to break the news to her. He should've just broke up with her a long time ago and saved her the grief of all the drama. Kenya eased away from the door un-noticed and sat back down at the bar. She had Dawson, the head bartender give her the entire bottle of wine. *"This shit is fucked up,"* was all that kept racing through her mind. *"O.T. ain't shit!"*

Kenya decided by her forth glass that it'd be better to keep this baby crap information from Paris as long as possible to spare her feelings. Considering the unstable depressing state of mind and constant stress that Paris had been dealing with, Kenya was terrified what would be her best friends response to all the madness that was going down. Luckily this was gonna be Chocolate Bunny's last week dancing.

◯

"Last call for alcohol!" The D.J. announced for the last and final time for the night.

It was damn near two in the morning and the club was slowly clearing out as the house lights came on. All the girls were going back to the dressing room to get changed and go home or where ever they planned on laying their head down at for the night. Some had boyfriends waiting, some had husbands and even a few had a bitch. Whatever the case was everyone was hauling ass to leave out.

"All right Addiction and Tight-N-Right, I'll see you ladies tomorrow." Boz held the door open and watched them to their rides.

"Hold up Boz, I'm ready to jet to!" Chocolate Bunny yelled out while struggling with her duffel bag followed by a loud talking Jordan.

"Yeah me to! I'll holler at yall in a few!" Boz saw Jordan and her woman kiss then drive off. Chocolate Bunny seemed to be enraged as she threw her bag to the pavement. "What kinda jealous ass hoe done did some treacherous shit like this?"

Boz walked over to investigate and found all four of Chocolate Bunny's tires slashed. "Damn! Who the fuck did you piss off?"

"You know how these bitches up here be hatin' on me because I clock dollars in this motherfucker!" Chocolate Bunny screamed across the parking lot to make sure that the rest of the dancers that hadn't left yet could hear exactly what she was saying. "Fuck you!" One of them replied as they all laughed at her misfortune and went on about their way.

Chocolate Bunny whipped out her cell, rolled her eyes and pushed number one on the speed dial.

"Hey Baby it's me!"

"Where you at?"

"I'm still at the club!"

"Why you still there, I was waiting for you?"

"One of these tramps done sliced my tires!"

"Just turn the sounds on and sit tight. I'm gonna send one of my street soldiers to find a nigga with a flat bed and come get you."

"Okay Sweetie, I love you!"

"I love you to! You and my son!"

Twenty minutes or so had passed and Chocolate Bunny was still sitting in her car waiting. Boz was chilling on the hood keeping her company. Kenya finally appeared at the door and waved for him to come inside. It was time to pay the security detail for the night and close up.

"You better come in the club and wait in there." Boz suggested as he opened the car door wide for Chocolate Bunny to get out.

"Yeah, you ain't never lied. I don't want nobody to kidnap my fine ass!" She joked as they both walked back into Alley Cats.

Kenya was going over the paper work and having each guy sign for his pay envelope. Boz had to do his job and okay each bouncer's nightly evaluation. As soon as Kenya was done with her part she focused on Chocolate Bunny who was sitting at the other end of the bar playing one of the poker arcade games.

"Hey girl, what's the deal?" Kenya interrupted.

"Nothing, just waiting for my Sweetie to send a tow truck to come rescue me."

"I'm sorry about your tires, but this gives me the opportunity to kick it with you about something."

"What is it Kenya?" Chocolate Bunny asked. "What did I do wrong now?"

"Nothing, I just need to talk. Give me a minute to finish things up and send the fellas home so we can have some privacy."

"Yeah whatever!" Chocolate Bunny put another quarter into the game to pass away the time.

Boz and the rest of the guys gathered their stuff and left out with a few beers in hand.

"Are yall gonna be all right?" Boz turned back asking before he started his truck.

"Yeah we good." Kenya waved him off. "Go ahead and bounce. See you tomorrow!"

She shut the front door making sure that it was locked. Kenya then took a seat next to Chocolate Bunny. "Listen, I swear to God that I'm not trying to be all up in your business but I think what you doing is wrong as a motherfucker."

"Excuse me, but what in the hell am I'm supposed to be doing Ms. Thang?"

"Don't play games. I was coming in the dressing room and heard what you said on the humble."

"What do you think you heard?" Chocolate Bunny snickered as she leaned back on the stool.

Kenya was getting angry at the brazen and heavy mouthed Chocolate Bunny. "So you about to have a baby huh?"

"And so what?"

Before Kenya could answer they heard a noise come from the rear of the club. Both of them froze looking at one another with a sense of fear because they knew for a fact that everyone had left. Kenya quietly made her way around to the other side of the bar grabbing the pistol that they kept on the bottom shelf. Two seconds later they heard the noise again.

"Whoever the fuck is back there, you about to catch some hot ones in the ass!" Kenya screamed out. "I'm not bullshitting! You best to come out!"

Chocolate Bunny and Kenya's mouths both almost dropped to the ground in disbelief when the person emerged out the dark shadow into the light. It was a wide red eyed, worn out and tired looking Paris.

She had her nightgown and slippers on while a huge 9mm pistol graced her side. Her hair was all over her head and her puffy face was full of tears. "It's me Kenya!" She dropped the spare club keys on the bar. "Why the hell is ya ass lurking like that?" Kenya lowered her gun. "I could've shot you."

"Damn, she's right are you crazy or what? Have you lost ya mind?" Chocolate Bunny jumped in.

Paris fingers tightly gripped the gun handle with animosity. "Don't say shit to me bitch!"

"Who the fuck is you talking to like that? I bout done had enough of you trippin' out whenever the fuck you feel like it!"

Kenya new that Paris was out her shit and didn't know what exactly she had planned, so she did her best to defuse the situation before it got out of hand. "Why don't we all just calm down?" She raised her hands in between Paris and Chocolate Bunny.

"Oh I'm good!" Chocolate Bunny replied, as she looked Paris up and down shaking her head. "I'm not the fool that's standing in a strip club in the middle of the night rocking pajamas."

"Paris, why are you here?" Kenya wondered. "And why aren't you dressed?"

"I didn't have time?" She was timid in her tone

Kenya threw her hands up in the air. "I'm confused as hell! What's going on? What's wrong?""

"This whore right here is what's wrong!" Paris pointed at Chocolate Bunny with her pistol.

"It'll be in your best interest to stop waving that motherfucker around before it go off, then it really will be some shit!" Chocolate Bunny put her hands on her hips showing no signs of fear of Paris.

Kenya stood back realizing that Paris was on some other type of shit and had snapped. "Just tell me what happened? I thought that you were at home sleeping?"

"I was until Jordan called me!" Paris wept.

It then hit Kenya what the fuck this whole scene was about. Jordan must've called Paris with that baby bullshit getting her fired up. "Listen Paris I was gonna tell you, but I just found out my self."

"Look, I hate to break up this soap opera, but I'll be out in my car." Chocolate Bunny blurted out.

"Bitch, I swear if you take one step that's ya ass!"

"Yeah okay Paris, can you just tell a chick what the fuck this is about, if you don't mind?"

Paris wiped her tears. "I heard you supposed to be having a baby?"

"Yeah and?" Chocolate Bunny put her hand on her stomach. "What about it? Is that okay with you?"

"Why the fuck would you think that the shit would be okay with my ass?" Paris fumed with anger.

"I ain't gotta clear my personal life with either of you two bitches. Yall buggin'!" Chocolate Bunny shifted her weight on one hip. "So deal with it!"

"So you ain't denying it?" Paris yelled nervously as her hand shook. "You're pregnant?"

Chocolate Bunny started moving her fingers acting as if she knew sign language. "Yes.. dumb.. bitch ..I.. am.. going.. to.. have.. a.. baby!" She dragged out each word while laughing. "Now..fuck..you!"

"Naw fuck you!!!" Paris raised the gun up and started to cry hysterically. "I can't take this bullshit no more! I'm sick and tired of yall playing me for a fool. Now you about to have his seed!"

Chocolate Bunny saw her chance and took it, bum rushing Paris causing them both to tumble to the floor. Kenya watched helplessly while the two rivals fought and wrestled for the gun. She couldn't tell who was getting down the best and had no intentions on trying to get a closer look, maybe getting shot by mistake. All Kenya could do, was clench her own gun tight and wait for the outcome.

◙

"Now what you crazy bitch! Where is all them empty threats at?" Chocolate Bunny had come out on the top and now had possession of the gun. "Talk all that shit now! So I can bust a cap in ya silly ass!"

 Paris was out of breath and her crying had gotten louder. Kenya had no choice but to put one up top and point her gun at a frantic Chocolate Bunny.

 "Why is yall hoes so worried about my son!" She panted as a sharp pain pierce throughout her lower side. Chocolate Bunny grabbed her side with her free hand and moaned out in agony. "His daddy is gonna.." Before she could get the words out another pain set in this time worse than the first.

"Son?" Paris whined. "You having a boy?'

"Oh my God!" Kenya pointed to the floor. "Look!"

Chocolate Bunny had dark blood running down her leg. It had started to form a small messy puddle, right beneath the spot where she was standing.

Her once white skirt was not only dirty from the filth that was on the floor, it was now soaked with her own blood. Reaching her hand up in between her legs she felt her pussy. When Chocolate Bunny pulled her hand back it was covered in thick blood. She smeared the blood on her skirt and went the fuck off. "You killed my baby! You killed my baby!" Her eyes grew wide with panic. "You dirty bitch!"

Chocolate Bunny pointed the gun at Paris' head and was about to pull the trigger as Kenya quickly let off two rounds knocking Chocolate Bunny off her feet slamming her battered body to the ground. The first one struck her dead in the stomach, more than likely taking the baby out the game for sure, while the other bullet found its mark in her collarbone.

Chocolate Bunny moaned softly as she took her last breath and slowly released all her bodily fluids.

I FUCKED UP

"Oh shit! I can't believe this!" Kenya lowered her gun taking a long deep breath. "That stupid bitch made me do that dumb shit!"

Paris just stood in the same spot, not moving and mouth wide the fuck open. Kenya tossed her pistol onto the bar and went to get the other one that was still in Chocolate Bunny's hand. Kenya then very carefully slid her finger off the trigger placing it with the other gun.

"What are we gonna do now?" Paris finally spoke.

"We gonna get rid of this black bitch, that's what!"

"I know, but how?" Paris was usually hard core, but lately she'd been punking out and scared of her own shadow.

"Just go in the back store room and get me that big roll of plastic that the painters left and the jug of industrial bleach." Kenya ordered. "And hurry up before this bitch bleeds even more on my floor."

227
Ms. Michel Moore

"Okay Kenya!" Paris ran towards the back.

They rolled Chocolate Bunny onto the plastic and drug her lifeless body over near the back door. Kenya had a scalding hot bucket of water and plenty of rags. Paris poured the strong bleach across the area and held her nose. It was supposed to be mixed with three parts water, but Kenya wanted it straight. Both girls' eyes burned as they scrubbed.

The club's floor was now spotless and there were no visible signs that a murder had just taken place. Kenya's car was already parked in the rear of the building so all they had to do was get Chocolate Bunny the hell out of there. It took ten long hard minutes of tugging, yanking and pulling to get her body stuffed and wedged behind the dumpster that had just been emptied the night before.

Paris took the plastic and balled it up placing it in a bag. On the way home she intended on disposing of it in someone else's garbage can on the other side of town. Kenya went back inside the club grabbing both guns off the bar and Chocolate Bunny's purse. She put them all in a small bag and doubled it.

After double checking the entire interior once again, she set the alarm and jumped into the car with Paris.

As they drove off they could see the flashing lights of a flat bed tow truck that was pulling into the club's parking lot.

"Damn! That was close!" Kenya kept glancing in the rear view mirror.

The ride to Paris house was silent after that. Neither of the girls said a word to the other. They were about one mile short of getting to their destination when a police car got behind the two murders. Kenya knew not to tell Paris that the cops were behind them because she knew that she would nut the fuck up and get them flicked for sure. Luckily at the next traffic light they hoe asses turned off.

When they got in Paris' driveway Kenya turned to her and stuck her hand out.

"What?" Paris squinted her eyes at Kenya.

"Give me your set of them motherfucking keys to Alley Cats, before your ass decides to come back in that bitch another night and lay a hoe to rest!" Kenya shook her head and laughed out loud.

Paris surrendered the keys and hugged her best friend. "Thanks Kenya. You saved my life!"

"Can you just go in there and chill for the night?"

◎

FACE FACTS

The rest of the way home Kenya's conscious started to kick in and go to work overtime. In a short amount of time she's been involved in covering up Swift's murder, disposing of Deacon's dead body and now actually committing the act of murder her self. *"I don't know how all this shit jumped off in the first place. All I was trying to do was make a little extra dough and get out the hood!"*

She pushed the remote and parked in the garage. Kenya found her way to the couch and plopped down. The condo was quiet except the on and off sounds of Storm in the basement snoring. Kenya assumed that London was sleep because it was so late. When London came walking down the stairs wide awake, it shocked Kenya.

"Oh my God! I'm glad you're up. I need someone to talk to! This shit is important. Come in the kitchen."

London was thrown off that Kenya wanted her to come in the kitchen. She thought that the shit was about to hit the fan about her and Storm having sex, so she sat at the table and braced her self.

Kenya put a plastic bag on the table and took her time pulling out the contents. The first two objects were both handguns. One of them had obvious signs of blood on the handle. The last thing Kenya quickly snatched out revealing was a designer purse.

"What is all of this?" London scanned the table puzzled as she watched her sister break down.

Kenya went on to explained exactly what events took place earlier, from the time her and Paris left the dinner. By the time Kenya was finish with her confession, London was caught up in her feelings. She was pissed, infuriated, enraged, disappointed and down right mad as a motherfucker at her twin.

"Why would you do something so stupid?

"Chocolate Bunny was gonna shoot Paris. What else was I supposed to do?"

"Paris had no business coming in Alley Cats acting all tough! That would have been on her!"

The twins arguing went on and on. London got up from the table to make some coffee and slightly lost her balance.

"What's wrong with you?" Kenya suspiciously asked with her eyebrow raised.

◉

PARIS

"What took you so long to come home?" Paris screamed at the top of her lungs. "Was you out shopping for baby clothes and shit?"

"What the fuck is your crazy ass talking about now?" O.T. stood in the doorway.

"I already know about you and that hoe having a baby so don't try to deny it!"

"What hoe you talking about now Paris!"

"That tramp Chocolate Bunny, that's who!"

"You know what? I wasn't gonna tell you this bullshit cause it wasn't none of your damn nosey ass insecure business, but you won't leave shit alone!"

O.T., after months of being secretive about his late night activities, filled Paris in. He explained the connection that he and Chocolate Bunny shared.

Hearing the full and complete story left Paris in shock over what she and Kenya had done. Paris had no choice but to tell O.T. what had taken place and that Chocolate Bunny was dead and stuffed behind the trash cans.

His reaction was anger as he socked Paris in her mouth and left out the house telling her that he was never coming home or back to her trouble making ass! Paris stumbled to the bathroom and opened the medicine cabinet. She twisted the top off a bottle of sleeping pills and swallowed a hand full. After all the shit she'd caused not trusting her Man, she welcome death, feeling that it was the only way out.

◎

DAMN!

While Kenya poured the coffee in the mugs, London looked in Chocolate Bunny's purse to turn off her cell phone that kept ringing. A thick folded set of papers were on the top and a few pictures. London read the first page, which was a purchase agreement and couldn't believe her eyes. "I think you need to see this." She motioned to Kenya. "Now!"

"Oh hell naw! What the fuck did we do!" Kenya yelled out with remorse.

The papers were a deed to Chocolate Bunny's new house. They had her government name on them as well as another, Mr. Royce K. Curtis. The picture was an ultrasound that also had Royce's name on it. "All this time Royce's old ass has been the one she's been fucking around with! Why didn't she just say that bullshit!"

Storm had woke up after a call on his cell phone from O.T and had been at the door listening and cut her off. "Because after the big fight that you and Royce had down at Alley Cats about me, all parties involved that it would be better for you not to know that he's our new connect. Plus it ain't really none of your business who she fucked with outside the club."

"Storm, I…" Kenya tried to explain.

"You know what Kenya? From day one right off rip I should've known that you was gonna be trouble. My brother warned me, but I wouldn't listen. Now it's about to be a street war because you and your sidekick Paris fucked the fuck up!"

Kenya went in to hysterics as she started throwing dishes against the wall and begging for Storm's forgiveness once again. She was crawling on her knees pleading with him not to leave her.

London was now pissed as she watched her own flesh and blood lower herself by this display. "Kenya! Get up off that damn floor! His ass ain't worth humiliating yourself like this!"

"Bitch! I bout done had enough of your instigating ass too! Why don't you pack your bags and get to stepping!" Storm ran up in London's face. "Get your ass the fuck out my house!"

"This is my sisters house to!" London fired back.

"Well Kenya, you gonna tell this bitch to be ghost or what?" Storm waited with a smirk on his face.

It grew quiet in the room as all eyes were on Kenya, who was breathing hard wiping the tears from her eyes. After a long pause she finally mumbled. "What did you say?" Storm demanded to hear.

"I said London, would you mind getting a hotel room somewhere until me and Storm figure all of this mess out?" Kenya failed to look at her twin sister.

"Oh, it's like that?" London was heated. "I've put my life on hold for you and now you're taking his side over mine! How could you?"

"Please London!" Kenya whined. "Please!"

Storm started to laugh. "You heard her bitch! Go pack your shit and leave!"

"Yeah okay!" London headed to her room to gather her things. "You two deserve each other!"

When she came back down Storm and Kenya were sitting on the couch talking. He was still dogging Kenya out, but stopped to taunt London. "Don't worry I already called your silly jealous ass a cab, you can go wait on the damn curb!"

Kenya was silent as London passed by and went into the kitchen to get something before struggling to drag her bag to the front door. Just as she opened the door the cab was pulling up and blew once. London looked back at her twin. "You sure about this? You're picking this dope dealer over me?" Kenya lowered her head in shame over her decision. After all they'd been through and stuck together the sisterly love and bond they shared was being torn.

"You know what it is bitch! Now kick rocks! Bye!" Storm held the door open. London turned around and pulled up her t-shirt exposing a secret of her own. Rubbing her stomach looking down she smiled. "Tell <u>AUNT Kenya</u> and ya' <u>DADDY Storm</u> bye!"

"What the fuck are you talking about London!" Kenya ran over to the door following her sister out to the cab. "What you mean Daddy Storm?"

London got inside the cab and shut the door rolling down the window. "Ask his ass what happened in the kitchen that night!" She pointed back at the condo where Storm was standing with his face buried in his hands having a flashback. *"Oh shit! That was her!"*

London instructed the cab to pull off leaving Kenya and Storm on the doorstep yelling loudly. "Where to Miss Lady?" The Cab driver inquired. London smiled as she opened one of her bags, which contained both guns and Chocolate Bunny's purse. "Can you please take me to Police Headquarters, the Homicide Division? I need to drop something off!"

I guess blood ain't thicker than water!

THE END…?

DO YOURSELF A HUGE FAVOR

AND

LOOK FOR THESE OTHER TITLES:

SAY U PROMISE!

BY -MS. MICHEL MOORE

ISBN# 0-9769991-02

GET IT HOW YA LIVE

BY- MS. MICHEL MOORE

ISBN# 0-9769991-1-0

&

COMING WINTER OF 2006

" *I'M OUT 4 SELF"*

SAY U PROMISE BOOKS

PO.BOX 38162

DETROIT, MICHIGAN

48238

313-443-7520

www.SAYUPROMISE.com

A BIG THANKS TO

HOOD BOOK

HEADQUARTERS

REPRESENTING

DETROIT

TO THE FULLEST

Ms. Michel Moore